L.J.A
F
STAR

FINNEY CO. PUBLIC LIBRARY
605 E. WALNUT
GARDEN CITY, KS 67846

D1396885

FINNEY CO. PUBLI

185969 udition for Death / by Al

DATE DUE

APR 22 1994	FEB 16 1994
JUL 31 1996	
Jun 16 1997	APR - 8 2000
AUG 3 1998	DEC - 4 2002
JUL 23 1997	
MAY 19 1999	AUG - 3 2004
AUG - 8 1999	
JUN 19 2000	

DEMCO, INC. 38-2931

AUDITION FOR DEATH

Other recent Avalon titles by Alice Sharpe:

NIGHT RUN
CHINA MOON
DESERT MAGIC
PARADISE BETRAYED
WEDDING BELL BLUES
A TIME FOR JOY

AUDITION FOR DEATH

•

ALICE SHARPE

AVALON BOOKS
THOMAS BOUREGY AND COMPANY, INC.
401 LAFAYETTE STREET
NEW YORK, NEW YORK 10003

© Copyright 1993 by Alice Sharpe
Library of Congress Catalog Card Number: 93-90596
ISBN 0-8034-9016-X
All rights reserved.
All the characters in this book are fictitious,
and any resemblance to actual persons,
living or dead, is purely coincidental.

PRINTED IN THE UNITED STATES OF AMERICA
ON ACID-FREE PAPER
BY HADDON CRAFTSMEN, SCRANTON, PENNSYLVANIA

This book is for my son-in-law,
Brett Jones,
the newest member of our family

Chapter One

" "That's okay, don't worry about it," Kristy Wilder said as she smiled through the pain of an elbow jabbed mistakenly into her side. The room was just too crowded, she decided. Theater people tended to wave their arms and take up more space than other people, and apparently the friends and family they brought along to parties suffered the same tendencies. There were even a few chain smokers—a breed Kristy had begun to hope were extinct—who were turning the air inside the sumptuous living room to something no air-quality board would ever approve.

To top it off, she was feeling let down now that the play was over and she'd never again assume the persona of Mary Mills, intrepid stepdaughter of paper tycoon, Lance Boggs. It had been fun while it lasted.

Kristy muttered hello to the large and slightly drunk husband of one of the other actresses; the man promptly spilled a drink on her foot. She escaped before he could drop to his knees and wipe up the mess with his vest, which he proposed to do, and ran straight into the broad chest of another man who put his hands on her arms and gently held her away.

"I'm so sorry," she said, looking up into the brownest eyes she'd ever seen, eyes the color of a sea otter's coat.

"No problem," the man said, dropping his hands.

The party was being thrown by the playwright and director of *Tree Tops*, James Winterberg. Kristy thought she knew everyone attending, as all the guests were either in the play or with someone who was, but this man was a stranger.

"You were very good as Mary," he said.

"Thank you. I just had a few lines."

"It was the way you said those lines."

Inordinately pleased, she said, "I wouldn't dare admit to *anyone* how many hours I spent working on sixteen little lines."

His lips curved into a delightful smile, and it occurred to Kristy that he'd probably come with Nancy Collins. It was well known at the theater that Nancy had broken up with her boyfriend of two years and that she was seeing someone new, but for once Nancy hadn't blabbed every detail of her personal life to anyone who would listen. However, if this man was actually the new love of Nancy's life, it was hard to believe she'd kept it quiet. He was exceptionally attractive.

"My name is Booker," the man said, extending a hand.

Kristy's hand was swamped by his. As she mumbled her name, she wondered at the fact that the casual brush of his skin against hers fired delicious little sparks up and down her spine. Amazing!

"I reviewed the play tonight for the *Tribune*," he

said, "and Mr. Winterberg was kind enough to ask me to drop by the party."

So he wasn't attached to Nancy. Kristy felt a smile tug on the corners of her mouth. "I'm glad you came," she said. "Is Booker you first name or your last name?"

"Only name," he said decisively.

She laughed softly. "I can tell there's a story there," she said, "but by the tone of your voice, I'll try to live with my burning curiosity. One question, though. Isn't it a little late to be reviewing *Tree Tops*? You do realize tonight was the last performance?"

"I know." He put his hand on her elbow and drew her close so their hostess, Regina Winterberg, heavily burdened with a tray of crab puffs, could squeeze her way through the crowd. He managed to swipe a couple of the little canapes and handed one to Kristy. They ate them while appraising each other.

"Now we need a glass of wine," he said.

"There's a keg out on the patio if you'll settle for beer."

"Sounds good," he said and followed her to the patio door.

It was still winter, though the first day of spring was less than a week away; the night was chilly, but the air was crisp and fresh with a hint of the ocean. Booker fetched two glasses of beer from the abandoned keg as Kristy settled on the waist-high rock wall which surrounded the patio. She dabbed what smelled like gin, courtesy of the large man in the vest, from the toe of her shoe with a tissue she found in her pocket.

The Winterberg house was located on the coast, atop

the cliffs, with a precipitous drop to the ocean below. Kristy could hear the waves thundering against the rocks at the base of the cliff and thought to herself it made a primitive kind of music which sang to a person's soul. Fanciful thoughts for an evening which was suddenly looking up.

"Be careful," Booker cautioned as he handed her a glass.

"I've been here in the daytime," she assured him. "The drop from this wall is only ten feet to a grassy slope. Up on that balcony"—and she pointed towards the second story of the house—"it's a different story. Fifty feet down, first stop, the rocks. No one sits on that railing!"

"I don't imagine," he said, shuddering. "Still, I have to admit I'd rather talk to you than watch you tumble off the wall and roll to the edge of eternity."

"Good point." She took a sip of beer, staring at Booker over the rim of the glass. "So, how come I've never seen you around? I thought I knew all the reporters, all two of them."

"I'm the new guy," he said.

"Great timing."

With raised eyebrows he asked, "What do you mean?"

"Someone from Los Angeles bought out old man Keeler. Of course, you already know that. Everyone in town is wondering what he's going to do with the paper."

"He's not sure," Booker said quietly. "He'll probably make a few changes, but basically I think he'll leave it alone."

Kristy regarded him with narrowed eyes which suddenly brightened. "You're the new owner, right?"

"Owner, publisher, editor, reporter."

"Head honcho?"

Booker shrugged, leaning against the rocks, his long legs crossed in front of him at the ankles. He was wearing a dark-gray suit and a burgundy tie. With his straight black hair and beautiful eyes, Kristy thought he looked more like a movie star than a newspaper reporter. Weren't reporters supposed to run around in worn corduroy jackets and jeans?

"Welcome to Cypress Hill," she said. "So, what did you think of *Tree Tops*?"

He shrugged. "I thought you were perfect. All those blond curls and China-blue eyes—you looked as innocent as a small child in the proverbial den of thieves. I can't tell you how delighted I was to walk into the room tonight and discover the hair is really yours and not a wig."

Kristy laughed. "Sounds as though you didn't enjoy the play much if my tiny role was the highlight of the evening."

He tilted his head, a subtle gesture Kristy had no trouble seeing, thanks to the subdued lighting placed every few feet along the house. His eyes were reduced to dark pools above his cheekbones. "You would have been the highlight in a Broadway production, Kristy Wilder," he said.

"My goodness, you do carry on," she said, making a joke of his compliment; the truth of the matter was that it touched her, thrilled her. How could she ever have thought this party was boring?

"And," he added, "I wanted to see this play because I hear Winterberg is going to direct another one very soon. I wanted to be able to compare them."

"So you're finally being honest—you didn't come just to feast your eyes on me. Well, I can live with that. You've heard about *Someday Soon*?"

"Just that Winterberg begins casting next week."

"That's right," Kristy said.

"I don't understand," Booker said. "How can Winterberg have another play ready to go so soon?"

"It was a local competition," Kristy explained. "Several people in the community submitted original one-act plays to the theater's board of directors, who chose three winners. Actually, they only chose two winners because James won twice. The other winner was a science-fiction play."

"I can close my eyes and picture it. There you are with five legs, three eyes, a tumble of green curls—"

Kristy laughed. "Shows what you know about science fiction. Besides, there weren't any women in the cast. I am thinking of trying out for a part in *Someday Soon*, though. I don't think anyone has seen the actual script yet, but from what I've heard, it pivots around a femme fatale named Lydia who metamorphoses into a tragic heroine when snubbed by her own true love."

Booker's brown eyes ignited with warmth. "You'll be an enchanting Lydia."

Kristy smiled. This guy sure knew what to say and how to say it. She hated to disillusion him, but facts were facts. "Hardly. Summer will get the role or at least she should. In my humble opinion, she's the best actress in town. She was one of my sisters in *Tree Tops*, the tall one with the reddish-brown hair.''

"What about the other sister?''

"Nancy Collins? She's good, too, better than me, anyway, but not as good as Summer.''

"Are you sure you're not just being overly modest?''

"I'm sure. Hey, you ought to try out for a part in the play. It can be a great way to get to know people in the community.''

"I can't act,'' he said.

"Neither can I. But it's fun to to get out there and try.''

"I'd be tempted if I thought it might involve a mushy love scene with you.''

Kristy took this lighthearted banter in the manner in which she figured Booker intended it and laughed. She was just about to respond when the door opened and Regina Winterberg stuck her head out.

"Kristy, it's about *that* time,'' she said, rolling her eyes.

"Time for what?'' Booker asked as Regina closed the door.

Kristy sighed and, setting her glass aside, scooted down from her perch. "Time for Rona and Duncan to sing their duet.''

"Rona and Duncan Barnett? The stars in tonight's play?''

"That's right.''

"And they sing?'' The way he said it implied he realized that even their acting left a lot to be desired. Kristy thought for a moment before answering. When she did, she was amazed to hear how honest her answer was.

"I doubt it."

"Now *that* sounds interesting," he said.

"I'd better explain. James asked them to perform tonight. I think what he had in mind was some little part of the play, but what they had in mind was singing. According to Regina, they've decided they're the next Steve Lawrence and Edie Gormé. I probably shouldn't admit this, but I haven't the slightest idea who Steve Lawrence and Edie Gormé are."

"They're middle-aged singers married to each other."

"Oh. Well, that figures, doesn't it? Anyway, James apparently caved in and arranged this little . . . musical interlude. Why am I telling the new owner of the local newspaper all this private stuff?"

"Because I inspire trust?" he said, a smile in his eyes.

"Hm—"

"Why would Winterberg encourage these people to sing at his party if no one thinks they can carry a tune?"

"I don't know. I guess just to be nice. He's like that."

Booker caught her arm before she could open the patio door. "I was just beginning to enjoy myself. Promise me we'll continue our discussion later."

"About the Barnetts? I really can't think why—"

"Not about them. About what we were talking about before Regina Winterberg came outside."

Kristy smiled internally, but she had the sneaking suspicion it made it to her lips as well. "Okay," she said, "but I really can't remember what it was we were discussing."

"It doesn't matter," he said softly, then reached in front of Kristy and slid open the door.

The hot room felt good after the nighttime chill. Kristy found a place at the end of the sofa, and to her delight Booker settled down on the arm next to her, his right hand behind her shoulders.

Rona and Duncan Barnett, whose identical red hair looked as though it came from the same bottle of hair dye, stood on an improvised stage—a huge hearth in front of an unlit fire. They were holding sheet music in their plump hands and assumed what Kristy often thought of as their "stage faces," intense looks of unearthly-like concentration.

Beside the hearth was a baby-grand piano, and on the bench sat Regina, her hands poised above the ivories. Her unenviable job was to accompany the Barnetts as they crooned out a selection of show tunes. She'd confided this to Kristy earlier in the evening; the two women now exchanged quick glances as James made his way to his wife's side.

As composed as Regina looked, he looked anxious. Well, you couldn't blame him, Kristy thought. It wasn't every day a host was called upon to murder his party by playing up to guests' egos.

James Winterberg, twenty years older than his wife, wore his fifty-one years well. He was tall and slender, partial to cashmere jackets and pipes he held between his teeth. He combed his graying hair straight back from his high forehead, and though Kristy didn't know him well, she thought him refined, distinguished, and kind. Besides writing and directing his plays, he also owned a chain of furniture stores, all located in Northern California and Southern Oregon.

"First, I want to thank each of you for coming tonight. It's been splendid having you in the company of *Tree Tops*, and I believe I speak for everyone when I say we'll miss that little play." James's rich, commanding voice hushed the crowd.

"But I'll begin casting *Someday Soon* within the week, and hopefully many of the same faces in this room will find parts in a new—and dare I hope?—even better play."

People cheered. Rona, probably assuming she'd capture the lead again despite the fact she was fifteen years too old, reached forward and hugged James.

He wriggled out of her effusive embrace and cleared his throat. "And now for the treat I promised you," he said, gesturing to the Barnetts. "As many of you know, Duncan and Rona have rehearsed a special musical treat for you tonight—"

"To try to convince you to write a musical," Duncan interrupted with a chuckle.

"I see. Yes, well, without further ado—"

"Wait a moment!"

Everyone turned to face the new voice. It came from Nancy Collins, who stood at the bottom of the stairs toward the back of the room.

Kristy hadn't seen Nancy since the makeup room at the end of the play, and the change between then and now was disturbing. She'd acquired a clinging white dress, unpinned her blond hair, and though she'd taken off her stage makeup, she'd replaced it with more street

makeup than she normally wore. The lipstick was deep
red, the rouge vibrant against her pale cheeks, but both
were outdone by the almost manic brilliance of her
blue eyes.

She weaved on the bottom stair and caught herself
on the banister. Was she drunk? As if to answer, she
raised an empty glass at the Barnetts and said, "You
guys can't sing!"

The room fell into a startled hush. Kristy finally said,
"Nancy, why not come sit here beside me?"

Nancy turned her unsettling gaze on Kristy. "Dear,
sweet little Kristy," she said, her clear voice loud, as
usual. "Always purer than the driven snow, aren't you?
Why do you suppose people always say we look
alike?"

Kristy, riveted to her seat with embarrassment, said,
"Just come sit down, Nancy."

"It's crazy, isn't it? I mean, you look like Alice in
Wonderland, and I . . . . Well, what would you say I
look like, Kristy? I know you'll be kind. You're always
so kind."

"Nancy!" James said.

Her gaze swiveled to the older man.

He regarded her with a stern expression. "Please,
go upstairs if you wish, but don't ruin the Barnetts'
duet."

"Do you honestly believe *I* could ruin *their* singing?" she asked, laughing.

James and Regina exchanged protracted, meaningful
stares, and a few quiet words passed between the Win-
terbergs and the Barnetts, whose faces were strained.
Regina's hands came crashing down on the keys for

the intro, the Barnetts began singing, and James moved away toward the stairs.

Kristy, reeling beneath an undercurrent of anger and dislike she hadn't known existed, was mortified by her exchange with Nancy. She'd always known she and Nancy weren't exactly soulmates, but until now they'd managed to maintain a veneer of politeness. She didn't hear the Barnetts; she just watched James march up the stairs and Nancy follow.

A warm hand settled on the top of Kristy's shoulder, and when she looked up, she found Booker staring down at her, understanding in his eyes, the proper degree of amusement—which put the whole episode in the right perspective—toying with his sensuous lips.

She smiled at him, and suddenly the Barnetts' dreadful voices came crashing into her consciousness.

The concert went on for what seemed like three eternities but was probably no more than ten minutes. What made things even stranger than they were, was the fact that Nancy's raised voice could sometimes be heard above the singing and the piano and, during lulls, resounded through the house.

Though Nancy's voice was clearly audible, no matter how hard Kristy listened, she couldn't make out any actual words. She felt terribly sorry for James Winterberg, who was apparently stuck in the same room with an irate drunk. Why was Nancy acting like this? She had a long and well-known history of emotional outbursts, but Kristy had never seen her overdrink before.

Rona Barnett stopped singing in the middle of a

medley of songs from *The Sound of Music*—surely a generous act on her part, Kristy mused—and stamped her foot as her eyes blazed at Regina.

"Really!" she snapped.

Regina stopped playing. She rose from the piano bench and faced her guests. "There's no use pretending we can't hear her, is there?" she asked.

Everyone started talking at once, and Kristy thought that as a coverup their many voices were better than the duet. On the other hand, almost anything was better than the duet.

"You actors," Booker said dryly. "Always emoting."

She punched his leg, which was the handiest part of his anatomy to punch seeing as they were still seated. "Don't bunch me in here with the likes of Nancy and Rona, please. I'm really a teacher."

"What grade?"

"High school creative writing and English," she said.

He smiled. "We have something in common, don't we? Besides the obvious, that is."

For several seconds they stared at each other, speculative smiles toying with their lips. Finally Kristy asked, "What do you mean, 'besides the obvious'? " She knew what he meant—mutual attraction. She just wanted to hear him say it.

Before he could answer, there was a crash from upstairs. Kristy sighed deeply and stood. "Excuse me," she said. Friends or not, someone had to take responsibility for Nancy tonight, and it didn't sound as though James were having much luck. She wondered if they should call Nancy's mother, and if they did, would Nancy's mother come? Ida Collins was seldom around the theater; on the few occasions when she had been there, she'd seemed tense and anxious to leave.

Kristy looked for Regina, but along with half the other people, she'd vanished. With a backward glance at Booker, Kristy climbed the stairs and found where everyone had disappeared to.

There was a huge crowd outside James's study door. There was no need for anyone to hold a water glass to the wood as Nancy's raised voice thundered through the wide hallway.

"There is no meaning!" she yelled loud enough to blister paint.

"Yes," James said, his voice much lower and harder to hear.

"I mean it. You've been a friend, and I appreciate it, but it's not enough. You don't understand. Tom is lost to me now, and I won't go on—I just won't. You can't make me."

Kristy felt her nerves jump. She looked at the other faces, but everyone seemed transfixed by the drama acting itself out on the other side of the heavy door. She moved closer.

"Don't be silly," James said, but there was no hint of urgency in his voice. Instead, he sounded bored and tired with the whole thing. "You're pretty," he added. "You're young—"

"As if that matters! You know it doesn't. I've lost the only man I ever loved. No, please, don't try to stop me."

And then it was silent, but even before this, Kristy

had decided enough was enough. She tried the door-knob, but though it turned, the door wouldn't push open. She applied the pressure of her shoulder, a man beside her leaning forward to help. The door scooted inward a foot, then refused to budge. Kristy squeezed through the narrow opening just as Nancy screamed, "I can't go on, I just can't!"

The room Kristy entered was James Winterberg's den. She gathered a quick impression of leather, wood, and books, but her eyes went straight to the man. He was standing in the open French doors, the heavily shadowed balcony behind him.

"Where's Nancy?" Kristy asked, her heart hiding in her chest, afraid of an answer.

James stared at her, his mouth half open.

"James! Where is she? What happened?"

"You didn't see?" he asked, his voice shaking.

"See what?"

He shook his head and glanced quickly over his shoulder.

Kristy was vaguely aware of a muted sound off to her left, but she didn't stick around long enough to identify it. She rushed past James onto the empty balcony.

"Nancy!" she screamed.

She heard James's agonized sob, and then he was beside her, looking down. Kristy's gaze followed his until she was able to pick out the whisper of white on the black rocks at the base of the cliff.

"No," she said, shaking James by his shoulders. "What happened? No!"

"She . . . she jumped," he said.

They both turned to face the room now crowded with party guests. James cried, "Nancy jumped. Heaven help me, I didn't think she'd do it. I didn't think she'd do it!"

Kristy helped him stagger into the room, where he collapsed on the chair behind his desk, his face buried in his hands. She noticed a half-full decanter of brandy on a tray along with a lipstick-stained wine glass and two smaller brandy snifters with amber rings in the bottoms. She thought to pour him a steadying drink but didn't. Regina burst through the silent gathering, gasping when she saw her husband's face.

Kristy walked back out on the balcony, the one with the treacherous drop to the rocky beach, her eyes easily picking out Nancy's white dress on the rocks below. She knew there was no way anyone could survive such a fall.

Chapter Two

"Is she dead?"

Everyone was whispering it.

Booker was suddenly beside Kristy. Considering how briefly she'd known him, it was incredible how comforting his solid warmth was.

"Call 911," he said to the crowd behind him. When no one moved, he barked, "Call for help. Get a search-and-rescue team out here."

Kristy caught his sleeve. "Booker, I don't think there's any way she could still be alive—"

"I know," he whispered. "But we have to try."

Before Kristy could get her bearings, Booker had found a couple of sturdy and sober men and with their help began descending the cliff, a rope tied around his waist, the two men on top of the cliff manning the rope which Kristy was relieved to see was also tied to the bumper of a 4 × 4 truck. She stood on the balcony watching as others turned flashlight beams on the rescue mission she knew in her heart was fruitless.

By the time Booker was hauled back, Kristy had made her way to the top of the cliff. Headlights from several of the parked cars had been turned on to illuminate the area. Kristy saw beads of sweat on Booker's face, streaks of dirt on his white shirt, mud caked on his black leather shoes. He looked at her and shook his head. "I think she died right away," he said, his voice soft.

It didn't come as a surprise, but Kristy felt huge tears well up behind her nose, and the next thing she knew, Booker had folded her in strong arms.

A. W. Booker hugged Kristy Wilder to his chest, her fragrant hair soft on his cheek, her body trembling. It had sickened him to lift the hand of the dead girl, to shine the flashlight in her face and find her eyes wide open but sightless. For all his years on city newspapers, he'd never actually been the first on a scene, never confronted death alone, especially on a rock ten feet above the pounding surf and fifty feet below other humans. Her body had been crushed by the fall, and he closed his eyes to shut out the details of an ugly death.

There was an insular quality to reporting, he reflected. A factor like a sheet of clear acrylic removed one from the immediacy of the scene, protecting with distance. Booker felt like running to his car for the camera he'd taken to the play, for his tablet of lined yellow paper, for his professional demeanor which would erase the image of the pretty blond girl dead on the rocks below. He held onto Kristy, as much for his benefit as hers, loosening his grip reluctantly when he heard sirens racing up the hill to the Winterberg estate.

Kristy faded into the crowd as Booker told the search-and-rescue party what he'd found below. The sheriff arrived as Booker shrugged on his suit jacket; then the coroner came, and while a team was organized to take an investigator down to examine the body and bring Nancy back up the hill, Booker retreated to his car for his camera, this time to cover a story, not hide behind an image, his newspaper instincts kicking in.

Kristy waited in the hall outside James's den until the sheriff mimicked the words leading up to Nancy's suicide; then she opened the door.

This time she was able to see the room more clearly. Two walls were covered with dark-wood paneling, a third held a low case, and a connecting door cracked open a few inches through which Kristy could see the edge of a gaily printed bedspread. The fourth wall was behind the desk and included the French doors, still open. The wind had turned chilly, and it blew into the room, but even its salt-tinged fingers couldn't dispel the lingering aura of tragedy.

James Winterberg stood by his desk, one hand gripping the wooden edge so hard his knuckles bulged white.

"You came in just like that?" Sheriff Fuller asked Kristy.

"It was hard to get through the door," she said slowly. "Something prevented it from opening."

The sheriff moved past her. He walked to the shadowed area to the right of the door; then he pulled the door toward him, leaned down behind it, and straightened back up, a suede slipper in his hand.

"This must have been wedged beneath the door," Fuller said.

"My slipper," James said woodenly. "I left it in here last night. Nancy threw it, not at me, in frustration."

"Is that what made the crashing sound we all heard from downstairs?" Kristy asked.

"No, that happened when she got up from her chair, picked it up, and practically threw it back down."

For a moment they all looked at the chair in front of Winterberg's desk.

The sheriff put the slipper aside. "Miss Wilder, Mr. Winterberg has told me what happened in this room. He's tried to remember exactly what Miss Collins said. I wrote it all down, and then I repeated it. You heard me while you were out in the hall?"

"Yes."

"And it sounded like a pretty accurate recreation to you?"

"Yes. In fact, it sounded exactly like what Nancy said."

"The curse of a playwright's ear," James mumbled.

"Now then," the sheriff continued. "We'll check this with the others, but you were the first person to enter this room after Miss Collins fell from that balcony. Tell me what you saw."

Kristy took a deep breath. "James was standing pretty much where he is now, kind of in the open doorway. I asked him where Nancy was."

And then she remembered the sound off to her left. She glanced in that direction now and found the bedroom door. Had someone else been in the room? She couldn't be sure the sound she heard was a door closing or opening, and besides, what did it matter?

"He didn't answer right away," Kristy continued. "I think he was in shock."

Sheriff Fuller was a short man with bristly black hair and gray eyes. He was wearing a black suit, and Kristy wondered if he'd been called here from a social engagement of some kind. He was also wearing a gold band on his left hand, and she thought about the wife whose dinner out had been cut short, or the party she stayed at alone while her husband came to do this sorry task. She shook her head, unclear on why her mind was wandering unless it was to avoid having to go to the rail and show how she looked down and saw Nancy.

"Then what happened?" Sheriff Fuller prompted.

"I don't remember exactly. I kept asking Mr. Winterberg what . . . what happened to Nancy. I think he nodded toward the balcony."

"Nancy ran right past me," James said. "I was sitting at the desk, and she was pacing back and forth, complaining about this and that . . . all I wanted to do was keep her up here until Rona and Duncan had a chance to sing their songs. I didn't really listen to her; in fact, after a while I barely heard her. I knew her voice was coming from over there by the shelves, and then she rushed past me. I could have stopped her if I'd understood, if I'd had any idea. I could have caught her, but I wasn't paying attention, heaven forgive me, I just wasn't paying attention."

"You shouldn't blame yourself," Kristy said. "We all knew what Nancy could be like."

The sheriff said, "Miss Collins was often distraught then, even suicidal?"

"From what I've heard around the theater, I'd say yes."

"I heard rumors, too," James said.

"Rumors?"

"It was said Nancy had tried in the past to kill herself," he said, his voice choking up.

"Is that what you heard, too?" Fuller asked Kristy.

"Yes, in the last week or so I heard the same rumors. Nancy hotly denied them. She said it was theater gossip, and I believed her. But tonight I heard her. She was terribly upset about losing her boyfriend."

The sheriff flipped through his notebook. "That would be Jim Turner?"

"He was her old boyfriend. I know nothing about the new one."

"She said Tom was lost to her," James said.

Kristy nodded. "That's right. I remember now. But I don't know anyone named Tom."

"Please continue," Fuller coaxed.

"Well," Kristy said as she took a deep breath, "I walked out onto the balcony, and I looked down."

The sheriff motioned for her to do it again, so Kristy walked past the two men and stepped out onto the balcony. She walked to the railing, which was about waist high. Had Nancy actually climbed on top of the metal structure? What had she thought about in the instant before she jumped? Did she regret her choice the second it was too late to change it, or was her mind deadened by alcohol?

Kristy looked down, as she had earlier.

The cliffs were well lit. A gurney was being hauled

upward, a body bag strapped securely within. Kristy turned away, her fist pressed against her mouth.

"Then I walked out and . . . looked," James said. "Kristy helped me back to my desk."

They walked back inside. As James sat down, Kristy looked at the brandy decanter. The little glasses were gone, but the empty wine glass—clearly Nancy's because of the vibrant red lipstick smudge on the rim—was still in place.

"And then I came in," a voice said from the doorway.

All three turned to face Booker, who stood just inside the room, a camera hung around his neck.

"Ah, Mr. Booker," the sheriff said. "The gentleman who called the police and organized a rescue operation."

"For all the good it did."

"The young lady was dead when you found her?"

"Yes," Booker said quickly and added, "Are you about done here? Miss Wilder looks dead on her feet. Winterberg doesn't look much better."

"We're just about done," the sheriff said. "Would all three of you say Nancy Collins had a drinking problem?"

"Yes," James said at the same time Kristy said no. When asked to explain, Kristy said that she'd never seen Nancy drunk before, though she'd certainly seemed so tonight. "Except for her voice," Kristy said, "she sounded fine."

"She was like that," James said. "We'd had . . . words about it before. She actually went on stage drunk one night. No one knew." His chin sank down against his chest from what Kristy guessed was a mixture of grief and fatigue.

"And how about you?" the sheriff asked Booker.

"I didn't know her," Booker said. "I just bought out Rudy Keeler and moved to town a few days ago."

"Then you're the new owner of the *Tribune*."

"Owner and editor, just like Keeler. I was at the theater tonight, and Winterberg asked me along to the wrap party. I saw Nancy Collins for the first time tonight. She wasn't a very big woman, about the same size as Kristy, and she certainly didn't sound drunk, but she was weaving."

"That's right," Kristy said, remembering that uncertain step on the stairs.

Fuller slapped his notebook closed. "Well, Booker, I suppose this suicide will make it into the paper day after tomorrow."

"No!" James said, suddenly alert.

Kristy saw Booker regard James with a curious gaze. He said, "Oh?"

"Keeler wouldn't have put this in print," James said. "I don't see why you have to."

"Well, for one thing," Booker said dryly, "I'm not Rudy Keeler. And for another, this is news."

"This is tragedy," Kristy said.

Booker shrugged. "At any rate, I haven't decided yet."

"Listen," James said, moving closer to Booker, "it's no secret in this town that I'm planning on running for mayor next term. News like this won't help me any."

Kristy touched his arm. "You have nothing to be ashamed of," she reminded him.

"But I am ashamed," he said, close to tears. "I could have saved the poor kid if I'd paid more attention to her."

"Don't torture yourself," Kristy said, glancing at Sheriff Fuller.

"She's right," Fuller said.

James shook his head, then buried his face in his hands.

"Maybe you could find his wife?" Sheriff Fuller suggested.

Kristy nodded, glad to have been given a helpful task. As she left the room, Booker touched her arm and smiled at her.

Kristy found Regina in the dining room, where she appeared to be storing freshly washed serving dishes in a pecan hutch. The two women smiled wearily at each other and embraced. They'd forged their friendship in the few months preceding Regina's marriage to James, when both of them had been new teachers at Manzanita High School. Kristy had been fresh out of college, a twenty-two-year-old neophyte, and Regina—five years older—a recent transplant from Denver, so the two had stuck together until Regina quit six months into the term to marry James Winterberg. Since then, their lives had led in opposite directions, but they tried to talk a few times a year, and during *Tree Tops* they'd seen each other at rehearsals.

"How's James holding up?" Regina asked.

"He needs you," Kristy said.

Finney County Public Library

Regina perched on the edge of a dining-room chair. "Oh."

Kristy studied the pale face so expertly surrounded with ash-blond hair, the tired droop of the thin shoulders encased in beige silk, the nervous hands stirring restlessly on the table. "Are you okay?" she asked.

Regina traced an absent pattern in the tablecloth with her fingernail. When she finally spoke, Kristy jerked to attention.

"It's no fun having some fruitcake kill herself in your home," she said.

Kristy was stunned with the cold tone of Regina's voice, to say nothing of her choice of words. She stared at Regina, uncertain how to respond.

"I told James she was trouble," Regina continued. "Right at the very start I told him, but he thought he could handle her, and now look."

Kristy nodded, half of her sympathizing with Regina, half of her thinking of Nancy's body smashed against the rocks. It hadn't been fun for her, either.

"I know I sound heartless," Regina said, her voice trembling. "It's just that. . . . "

"What?" Kristy prompted.

"I don't know, Kristy. It's just that . . . well, no one knows this yet. I don't know why I'm telling you, except that we used to be friends."

"We still are," Kristy said automatically.

"Yes. Well, perfect timing as usual. I'm pregnant."

"Oh, Regina! James must be thrilled."

"I meant what I said. I haven't told a soul, not even James."

"Why?"

Regina shrugged. "I was waiting for the right time. And now this."

Kristy said, "Nancy's suicide doesn't have anything to do with you and your baby."

Regina studied her hands. At last she said, "I guess not."

"Of course not."

Regina looked unconvinced, and Kristy didn't understand why. She said, "After a death, a new life is doubly precious. Tell James—you'll see."

"Not yet," Regina said anxiously. "Promise me you won't tell a soul. I want time to pass between this . . . this mess and my announcement."

"Of course I won't tell him. I'll do whatever you want."

They both stopped talking as they heard a commotion from the front hall.

"Now what?" Regina asked as she wearily rose to her feet. Kristy followed her to the front door where they found a deputy trying to keep a red-faced man wearing jeans and cowboy boots from coming inside.

"I tell you, son, I'm coming in there, and that's all there is to it!" the man hollered.

Though both men were approximately the same height, the newcomer must have outweighed the deputy by fifty pounds. He was wearing a blue and gold cowboy shirt with pearl buttons and a huge tooled-silver belt buckle. Kristy thought he looked about forty, with fair wavy hair and a thick neck.

"You aren't coming in here until I talk to the sheriff," the deputy insisted, his thin arm blocking the door.

"What is this?" Regina asked.

The man stopped struggling with the deputy and looked at Regina. "Name's Hook," he said. "Charlie Hook. I was supposed to meet my girlfriend here. What's going on?" he asked, waving his arm toward the police cars. "I passed an ambulance going down the road."

"There's been an . . . accident," Regina said, struggling over the word.

"Someone hurt?"

Regina bit her lip. Kristy heard footsteps and looked up to see Booker and the sheriff descending the stairs. The sheriff said, "Butterworth, what in tarnation is all the commotion down here?"

Deputy Butterworth nodded toward Charlie Hook. "He was trying to come in here, Sheriff. You told me to keep folks out—"

"There something I can help you with, mister?" the sheriff asked.

Charlie Hook sighed. "I just want to pick up my little gal, that's all," he said. "Been singing with a band over at the Lonesome Tortoise. Nancy said to meet her here. Just point me in her direction, and I'll get out of your way."

"Nancy Collins?" Regina gasped.

"That's right. Prettiest thing you ever saw, but I guess you know it if you're her friends."

"Let me get this straight," Fuller said. "You're Nancy Collins's boyfriend and your name is Charlie?"

"That's right. Hey, what's going on here?"

"Did she ever call you Tom?"

"Of course not. Listen here, Sheriff, with all due respect, what's this got to do—"

The sheriff interrupted. "Come with me, sir," he said. Deputy Butterworth finally dropped his arm, and Charlie Hook came into the house, sparing a smug look for the deputy. The sheriff said, "Mrs. Winterberg, may I use your living room for a moment, ma'am?"

Regina nodded.

As Sheriff Fuller closed the double doors behind Charlie Hook, Regina began softly crying.

Kristy put her arm around her friend's shoulders. "It's going to be all right, Regina."

"It's just all so awful. . . ."

"I know. Why don't you go upstairs to James?"

"Yes," Regina said, wiping the tears out of her eyes with shaking fingers. "Remember, you promised," she whispered.

Kristy nodded and said, "Trust me."

"I've got to think," Regina mumbled almost to herself and began climbing the stairs.

Booker cleared his throat. Kristy had almost forgotten he was still there. She twirled around to face him.

"Tell me you need a ride home," he said softly.

"Actually, I do. My ride left hours ago," she said.

"Good." He took her arm and steered her outside.

"It's hard to believe we only met a few hours ago, isn't it?" Kristy asked through a yawn.

"It's been a pretty intense few hours," Booker said. He'd pulled up in front of Kristy's house and turned off the engine, and now they sat staring out at the dark road, too weary to move. A streetlight overhead partially lit the interior of the car.

Booker was thinking of the way he'd like this evening to end. Assuming she was willing, he'd like to gather Kristy into his arms again, feel her soft, golden curls against his cheek, taste her lips. He wanted to dive into those forget-me-not blue eyes, run his fingers over the incredibly fine texture of her skin, feel her soft arms circle his neck, resume the playful flirtation they'd indulged in on the patio.

But he couldn't. He could sense the moment was wrong, and in his heart he knew it was wrong for him, too. As a matter of fact, maybe in some perverse way it was better this tragedy had shaken him out of the easy little romance he'd envisioned when she first ran into him. He had a weekly newspaper to get back on its feet and an unlucky way of falling for the wrong woman at the wrong time. The last thing he needed was to become infatuated with Kristy Wilder. It was easy to tell she was the kind of woman to demand more than witty banter; sooner or later she'd want something he wasn't prepared to give. He'd been that route once before, and he'd given and given—and look where it had left him: divorced.

He glanced at Kristy out of the corners of his eyes and felt most of his resolutions weaken. He suddenly remembered the sight of her perched on the rock wall, her skirt fluttering in the mild breeze, her arms wrapped around herself for warmth, and he felt an unfamiliar wave of protective tenderness wash through his heart. That same heart was now flashing danger signals to his brain. He cleared his throat.

"I haven't said it yet," he began, "but I'm sorry about your friend."

She turned her gaze to him. "That's the part that makes me feel the worst," she confided. "The awful truth is, I didn't particularly like her. I can't tell you how guilty it makes me feel that while I'm dreadfully sorry Nancy was so miserable, she felt as though she had to end her life, I'm also angry she did it in James and Regina Winterberg's house. I keep thinking she must have enjoyed the whole thing—you know, having everyone in a turmoil, being the center of her own little tornado. I keep thinking it just all got out of hand because she was so drunk."

How anyone could look so young and vulnerable and sound so worldly-wise and weary! "Then you don't think Nancy Collins intended to commit suicide?"

"I don't know," Kristy said. "She was just so involved with herself. Do people like that really kill themselves?"

"I haven't the slightest idea, but judging from what's happened tonight, I'd say they sometimes do."

"I wonder," she said, closing her eyes and resting her head against the cool window.

"What do you mean?"

"I wonder if she just went too far," she explained, yawning into her hand. "I wonder if the whole thing was just an awful mistake."

"What do you make of the boyfriend?" Booker asked.

"That poor man."

"Do you suppose she had two new boyfriends, Charlie Hook and this Tom she killed herself over?"

"It wouldn't be impossible," Kristy said, yawning again.

"You're dead tired."

"I know. And I'm talking too much. You're very easy to talk to, aren't you? How about it, Booker—are you a newsman first, or a gentleman?"

"You don't think I can be both at the same time?"

"I don't know," she said, "but until I find out, I guess I'd better learn to keep my mouth shut."

"Pity."

"Are you going to write about tonight?"

"I haven't decided," he said.

"Hm—Well, thanks for the ride. I'm sure I'll see you around town—"

"Sure," he interrupted. He got out of the car and saw Kristy to her door, ignoring the way he longed to kiss her good night. She spared him a smile that did little warm things to his heart, and he left, determined to put some distance between himself and a woman he suspected was going to be nothing but trouble.

Kristy awoke the next morning with a throbbing headache, a leftover, she decided, from the horrible events of the night before. As she stared at the ceiling above her bed, she regretted saying she hadn't liked Nancy. For one thing, it wasn't that easy. While she didn't subscribe to the idea that death wiped away a person's faults or endeared the unendearable, she did realize that death would have sanded smooth the abrasive edges of Nancy's personality if it hadn't been for Regina's and James's obvious distress and what must now be the broken heart of a singing cowboy named Charlie Hook; Nancy Collins, true to form, had chosen a very selfish means of dying.

Or maybe, Kristy admitted privately, anger was easier to cope with than grief.

Still, she wished she hadn't said it, especially not to Booker. Rudy Keeler had been a big bear of a man, lovable and almost cuddly. Booker wasn't. While he was easily the most interesting man she'd met since college, he was also fresh from a big city, and she had the gut feeling that his mind was like a tape recorder, storing everything it heard. Hadn't he seemed kind of quiet as they walked up the path, his easy banter strangely absent? Was he busy thinking about all the foolish things she'd said?

Embarrassed and strangely lethargic, she tried closing her eyes and going back to sleep. She wouldn't think about Booker; after all, he was virtually a stranger, and it was unlikely their paths would cross again.

At least it was Sunday, she mused, so she wouldn't have to face her students for a day. Had someone told Nancy's mother? She should have volunteered, but the police must have imparted the bad news by now. Kristy wondered how Ida Collins would take her only child's death, especially since it was a suicide. There was something about a suicide, a residual guilt and humiliation for the family and friends left behind. Could they have done something to prevent it, said something, or, even worse, had they inadvertently caused such massive despair? Even James Winterberg was questioning his behavior, regretting what he hadn't done.

The ringing phone finally dragged her from her bed at half past ten. The call was from her mother in Oregon. Though Kristy didn't tell her what had happened the night before—her mother didn't know Nancy—there was comfort in the familiar voice.

"I've been shopping over the telephone again," her mother said after the preliminaries. "This time I bought something for you. I had it shipped directly to your house, so you should get it in a few days."

Kristy, remembering the last such purchase, a full-length fake fur coat that looked real enough to make Kristy uncomfortable due to her firm belief in animal rights, shuddered. "You shouldn't have, Mom." The coat was still hanging in its plastic bag in her closet.

"What's a mom for? And when you get the lead in the next play, we're all coming down to see you."

"You're going to be driving a long way to hear your firstborn utter a dozen lines," she warned. "There are three of us the right age for the lead. The other two are better and more experienced than I."

It wasn't until the words left her lips that she realized there were only two of them now, herself and Summer Sanders. Nancy was gone. . . .

"Are you still there?"

"What? Oh, sure, Mom."

"Well I don't care if you get the lead or not. Do your father good to get away from the sawmill for a while. And Randy will take any excuse to get a few days off school."

"Don't tell me that," Kristy said. "Remember, I teach kids Randy's age. Tell the little squirt hi for me."

"Will do. Kristy, are you sure nothing is wrong?"

Kristy smiled to herself. Leave it to her mother. "Nothing you can help with," she said honestly.

"Now, Kristy—"

"You're awfully good at this, aren't you?"

"Years of practice. What's up?"

"A casual acquaintance of mine has died. I really don't want to go into it."

"Young like you?"

"I'm afraid so."

Her mother made consoling sounds. Even after Kristy hung up the receiver and popped a couple of aspirin into her mouth, she heard those sounds and felt double-faced. Why hadn't she been able to like Nancy Collins?

The *Cypress Tribune* was a modest paper with a modest circulation. It was housed in a gray brick building along Main Street; its main claim to fame was the wisteria vine someone had planted in the dim past and which now climbed the outer wall, framing the doorway and large front window. In the late spring, huge drooping clusters of purple flowers covered the entire newspaper frontage, making it a landmark of sorts.

The wisteria hadn't been blooming when Booker first looked into buying the paper from Keeler; in fact, all that had been visible of this springtime phenomenon was a tangle of dry brown vines. Booker had been more than a little shocked when he rolled into town three months later and found his newspaper office looking more like a beauty shop than a serious place of business.

Approaching it now, and for only the third time, he felt a budding sense of approval. Los Angeles newspaper buildings did not come wrapped in flowers, so these made a visible statement about his decision to leave the rat race behind.

Who would ever thought investing in a scheme to print a television guide for satellite users could have led to such wealth and, even more importantly, the freedom to pursue his long-time dream of owning and running a small-town paper? It had been a gamble which paid off; not all of them did. Not that he was much of a gambling man, but when his long-time friend Buddy Wright had pleaded for capital, he'd had a hunch Buddy was onto something. He'd had no idea it would pay off so handsomely.

He unlocked the door and entered the room, pausing to switch on the lights before crossing behind the long counter to his office. The production room was down a long hallway on the left side of the building. He flipped on his office light, then went back into the main room, looking for a book he'd left on the typesetter's desk.

His domain. Booker looked around the modest enterprise and smiled. He kind of liked it when Karen, the ad-slash-counter person, and Frank, his one and only fully employed reporter-slash-typesetter, were gone. He went back into his office and sat at his desk, his gaze settling on the stack of mail from his corresponding reporters. Seven envelopes representing everything from an advice column to gardening advice.

Someone had to type them into the computer. The someone was him.

Someone also had to decide exactly how much to say about Nancy Collins's plunge over James Winterberg's balcony railing. Discretion said keep it short and simple. On the other hand, Winterberg was a prominent citizen about to run for mayor. One thing was certain: it wasn't Booker's way to bury a story.

His mind immediately flashed back to the night before. Would Kristy Wilder understand all this?

Who cares if she doesn't? he thought in a fit of defiance.

Kristy tapped on the box-office window, right under the crisply painted words, *Cypress Hill Repertory Theater*. Greta Sanders looked up from her tasks and smiled as she stood. When she opened the door, she said, "What are you doing here today?"

"I need to collect my stuff," Kristy said. "The stage door is locked."

"Henry must be out on one of his errands," Greta said. Henry and Greta were long married, a comfortable couple with lots of smile lines on their weathered faces. Their granddaughter was Summer Sanders.

"I thought Hank Roscoe was in there making sure all the costumes were ready to be sent to the cleaners."

"If he's upstairs in the costume room, he wouldn't have heard me pounding on the stage door," Kristy pointed out. Hank Roscoe was the costume designer, had been for fifteen years. It was his responsibility to come up with the costumes which would reflect the various characters' personalities, a job he performed brilliantly.

"That's right, he wouldn't. I'll let you in," Greta said, digging around on her cluttered desk for the theater keys. She was the box-office manager, husband Henry the house manager.

The theater had been converted from a movie house twenty years before. They'd kept the lobby, changed the projection room to a light-and-sound booth, gutted the inside of the theater, replacing the old seats with comfortable new ones, and built up a stage. Greta locked the door behind Kristy and went back to her office while Kristy parted the lobby curtain and looked upon the stage.

The cast and technical crew had struck the set the night before, right after the last performance and before the wrap party. All that was left of *Tree Tops'* beautiful, old-fashioned parlor was a pile of lumber and a loveseat constructed out of foam and plywood. The lumber would be stored in the building out back to be recycled into the next set, for *Someday Soon*. The loveseat had been promised to a local merchant who wanted to use it to display her handmade dolls in the big front window of her downtown store. Since the loveseat wouldn't stand up to anything more vigorous than inanimate dolls, it was a perfect match.

It was impossible to face the stage and not think of Nancy Collins strutting downstage, her lines less polished and rehearsed than her body movements. She'd been infuriating at times, but she'd also been intensely alive. Kristy suddenly realized Greta hadn't mentioned anything about Nancy's suicide, which meant she probably didn't know yet. Summer hadn't been at the party, so she was probably unaware, too.

Kristy wasn't sure if she wanted to be the bearer of such bad news; on the other hand, better it should come from her and not the local grapevine. Before she left, she'd tell Greta and let Greta tell her granddaughter. Summer and Nancy had once been close.

"Hard to believe she's gone, isn't it?" a male voice said from behind Kristy. She twirled and found herself facing Hank Roscoe. In his early fifties, with a slender frame and short gray hair, Hank was a theater favorite. His arms were full of costumes Kristy assumed he was taking to the dry cleaners. He'd been at the party the night before, and Kristy didn't have to ask who he was referring to.

"It is. She was so vibrant."

"Especially last night," Hank said. "When you saw her on the stairs, did you ever imagine you were looking at a woman so desperate she'd throw herself off a balcony a few minutes later?"

"I hadn't thought of it exactly like that," Kristy said.

"She was a better actress than I ever gave her credit for," Hank said. "Well, I'll be on my way. Hope I see you in *Someday Soon*," he added.

"I'll audition, but who knows?" Kristy called out after him. She walked down the left side aisle. To the left of the stage was a curtained doorway. She parted the curtain and quickly climbed the four stairs that led to the backstage area.

The first thing she came upon was the stage manager's desk, a small blue light bulb burning above it.

She walked past that and entered the area they called the dressing room; in actuality, it wasn't a room at all but a long, wide hallway open on both ends. Modesty wasn't a highly priced virtue for an actor, but for those who insisted on it, a flight of steep stairs led to a small room above the dressing room which afforded some modesty—there were several gaps in the floorboards—and suffocating heat as well.

Behind the dressing room, through a door set at an angle which kept light from penetrating the backstage darkness, was the makeup room. This consisted of two long counters with brilliantly lit mirrors above and numerous chairs below. Shelves held bottles of tinted skin tones. Next to the shelves was a row of small lockers, newly installed after an actor on the previous show complained someone stole his good watch. Kristy halted in front of number three, twirled the combination, and opened the door.

Crammed inside were a red sweater, black sweatpants, two apples, three paperback books, worn jogging shoes, her own makeup kit, and a briefcase engraved with the initials N.C.

Kristy dropped all her belongings into a paper sack and then lifted out the briefcase.

She could almost hear Nancy's voice: "My locker is too blasted full. Put this in yours."

"I'd like to," Kristy had said, "but I don't have room."

"You'll find room," Nancy had insisted, shoving the briefcase toward Kristy. "I'll get it from you tomorrow." And then she disappeared out the doorway.

There had been no tomorrow for Nancy, and now

Kristy was somewhat ashamed of begrudging her the storage space. She was also unsure what she should do with the briefcase now that its owner was dead. Undecided, she took it with her.

With a final look at the makeup room, she flipped off the lights and made her way back to the box office and Greta Sanders.

Chapter Three

" "This is touchy-feely stuff, Miss Wilder."

The complaint came from Rob Stevenson, who at fifteen years was acutely uncomfortable writing about his feelings.

Kristy said, "Give it a try, Rob. You may surprise yourself."

"You may surprise everyone," Tanya Rollins said, poking her classmate's back with the eraser end of a pencil.

Rob slid down in his desk so that his legs stuck out into the aisle. He glared at the empty paper in front of him, his mouth set in a scowl. "I just can't do it," he muttered.

Kristy leaned back against her desk and thought. Finally she said, "The assignment is to write about the most poignant thing that's ever happened to you. First of all, do you know what poignant means?"

"Yeah."

"What?"

"You want to know about something touching or emotional," he said in such a way that half the class—mostly male, Kristy noticed with chagrin—laughed.

"Right. For people your age, that sometimes means the death of a grandparent."

"Two alive, two I don't even remember," he said smugly.

Kristy nodded. "Okay. How about your first kiss?"

The classroom dissolved into hoots and hollers. Rob's face suffused with red.

"Or the time your little sister picked a flower for you, and don't tell me you don't have a little sister because I saw her on back-to-school night. Or the time your parents told you they were proud of you or you won first prize at the science fair or a girl you like offered to carry your books. Are you getting my drift?"

"Yeah," he mumbled.

"This may sound sexist, but sometimes boys hide behind this macho thing," Kristy heard herself saying. "They pretend they don't have any feelings. If they pretend long enough, they can wake up one day and discover they're so out of touch with themselves, they've become strangers to their own emotions."

She looked out at the sea of twenty-five faces, all directed her way, and smiled. "So," she said, "think with your head and your heart, and you'll come up with some incident that touched you and then write about that. And write about it your own way, okay? Does anyone else have a question about our subject?"

No one said a word. Kristy sat down behind her desk and began grading papers. Her mind wandering, she noticed a speck of dirt under her fingernail, a tenacious leftover from her efforts Sunday afternoon to thumb her nose at winter and plant marigolds. She flicked it away and looked up to see Patricia Hooper getting up from her desk. Kristy looked back at the papers; if there was one student in the world she could do without at this moment, it was Patricia Hooper. Maybe Patricia would get the hint.

The young girl came up to the desk and waited patiently by Kristy's elbow.

"Question?" Kristy asked.

"Not about the paper," Patricia said. She was a quiet, plump girl who rarely smiled, though she didn't seem particularly unhappy. She just didn't smile much. She leaned very close, so close her stale breath felt warm on Kristy's cheek, and said, "I heard you were there when Nancy Collins killed herself."

Kristy pushed down on her pencil so hard the lead broke. She looked up quickly.

"My mom heard it from Nancy's cousin's hairdresser," Patricia explained. "She said Nancy killed herself over a guy named Tom."

"Good heavens!" Kristy said.

"It's a small town, Miss Wilder."

"I guess it is. Well, Patricia, yes, I was there. As for what happened, well, that I didn't see."

"Nancy's cousin's hairdresser said the cops questioned you, though. She said—"

"I'm sorry, but I really don't want to talk about this."

"But you didn't like her, did you? I mean, after what she said to you at the party about her boyfriend saying you were a goody two-shoes—"

"Patricia! Honestly. Your facts are distorted. Please, sit down now and try not to think about this tragedy, and for heaven's sake don't gossip about my supposed role in it.''

"But—"

"I insist.''

Patricia stuck out her lower lip and walked slowly back to her desk.

Kristy stared at the paper in front of her and wondered how much of Cypress Hill was gossiping about Nancy's suicide. She wondered if Booker would actually write about it in the Wednesday paper. Surely he wouldn't—what was the point? She knew nothing of his background except that he'd come from Los Angeles; hopefully he'd realize Cypress Hill was a town of neighbors, that good taste dictated as little news as possible when a death was a suicide no matter how anxious the populace was for all the gory details. But he'd been so vague about it. . . .

"Hey, Miss Wilder," Rob said suddenly. "I thought of something. My mom ran over our cat last Saturday. I got pretty choked up about it, too.''

"How touching," Kristy said and resumed grading papers.

That night, Kristy phoned Ida Collins and got a woman who identified herself as Ida's sister.

"Ida is awfully torn up over this, I can tell you that," the woman said.

"Do you think she'd mind if I came over to her house for a few minutes? I have something of Nancy's I'd like to give her.''

"She won't care one way or the other," the sister said.

Ida's house was located on the edge of town where the road began cutting inland. Since she lived only a mile away, Kristy walked, the briefcase swinging by her side. It was a very nice leather case, well balanced and not too heavy.

The house had been a real beauty once, but time, weather, and apathy had taken their toll. Kristy made her way along the neglected front walk and knocked on the door. The blare of the television was instantly subdued, and then the door was opened by a woman who looked so like Ida that for a second, Kristy thought that's just who she was.

"You must be the girl who asked about coming over—Kristy something or the other."

"Yes—"

"I'm Ida's twin sister, Anne Argot. You just call me Anne," the other woman said, standing aside so Kristy could come into the house. She was a small, wiry-looking woman nearing fifty, her grayish hair cut short and straight, her expression open and direct. It was that expression which most differentiated her from Ida Collins, who was seated on the sofa staring listlessly at the television set, the volume turned way down but the picture intact.

Ida looked up as Kristy approached her. There were no tears in the dark eyes, but there was no life, either. The older woman looked away quickly, her gaze straying back to the television.

Kristy wasn't sure what to do. She looked toward Anne, who sighed.

"She ain't been right since that girl of hers killed herself."

"She didn't!" Ida hissed without looking up.

Kristy swallowed and wished she could evaporate from the room.

" 'Course she did, Sis, and you just better get used to it. Lots of people heard her talk about it, and that poor man had to watch. You can't hide in here staring at the fool TV all the time 'cause you're afraid of what people are saying. Can she, miss?"

Kristy said, "It must be very difficult."

Ida slowly turned her gaze to Kristy. "You were there," she said.

Kristy nodded, gripping the briefcase handle until her knuckles were white. Please, don't ask me about it, she silently pleaded, but wasn't surprised when Ida did.

"Sit down here. Tell me what happened. Tell me what my little girl said. Every word. It wasn't like the sheriff said it was; tell me it wasn't."

Kristy sat down on the ottoman facing the sofa. She set the case aside and folded her hands together, meeting Ida's bewildered stare straight on. "With all my heart, I wish I could," she said softly. "But I can't. I'm terribly sorry."

Ida fixed her with a menacing stare. "I don't care," she blurted out. "I won't believe it, I just won't. Nancy was a survivor, not a quitter. She wouldn't throw herself off a balcony and die like that, not over some man—I know she wouldn't." Ida's face crumbled into a new mask of grief. When she looked at Kristy again, her eyes were blurred by tears. "She wouldn't, she just wouldn't."

"I'm so sorry," Kristy said softly, feeling more inadequate than she'd ever felt before.

Ida shook her head miserably. "I'm not staying in this town," she cried. She got to her feet and walked toward the hallway, her movements stiff, as though she'd forgotten how to use her legs. When Anne tried to comfort her, she shook her away and hurried into the shadows. A moment later Kristy heard a door close.

Kristy looked at Anne. "Maybe I should have lied," she said softly.

"No," Anne said. "I shouldn't speak ill of the dead, especially since Nancy was my niece and everything, but the truth of the matter is the girl caused her mama nothing but grief from the time she first learned how to wiggle her behind. Ida is just going to have to get over it. You ask me, she's acting like this 'cause she and Nancy didn't get on so hot the last couple of years. I think that makes it harder in some ways 'cause you keep thinking about what might have been, blaming yourself for how things just weren't right. That and the fact that Ida never touched a drop of liquor in her life and it's eating her up that Nancy got drunk so often."

"Who told her that?" Kristy asked as she stood.

"Rumors. This town of yours is full of them. Then the sheriff called today and gave us the results of the partial autopsy they did. Seemed Nancy was full of booze when she took off over that railing."

Kristy nodded. No surprise there.

"Anyway, child, is that briefcase what you brought to give to Ida?"

Kristy picked it up. "It was Nancy's. I was storing it for her."

"Funny thing, ain't it, but Nancy didn't strike me as the briefcase type. If it were up to me, I'd tell you to keep the darn thing; Ida wants me to put an ad in the paper. She says she's selling off everything in the house, moving away. I only hope I can convince her to move back to Spokane with me. She's got nothing here anymore. Do her good to get away, don't you think?"

"It couldn't hurt," Kristy said sincerely.

"But still," Anne added as she opened the door for Kristy, "I have to agree with Sis on one point. Nancy never seemed like the kind of girl to kill herself, did she?"

"No," Kristy agreed, well aware the same thought had been chasing its tail around in her own mind for the better part of two days.

Booker was working late at the paper that night. He'd long since sent everyone else home, but to get the paper to the printers for afternoon publication the day after tomorrow, he'd have to put in a long evening.

For instance, he mused as he read the material sent in by Adelaide Thomas for her feature, Ask Addie. Should he leave her answer intact or condense it? He read both the letter and response aloud:

Dear Addie—My boyfriend says he loves me but he keeps dating other girls, too. He says there are more women in the world than there are men and it's his duty to spread himself around, whatever that means.

He says I'm selfish. What would you do? It was signed, *Ain't Happy Being One of the Pack.*

Addie answered: *Dear Ain't Happy Being One of the Pack—Your boyfriend is obviously immature and uncaring. He is using you as a home base while he plays the field and expecting you not only to allow it, but condone it as well. Then he blames you for being selfish when it's really him who's selfish. He's using you, no doubt because he never had a strong father figure. I'd suggest counseling for the both of you as a couple. If he won't go, go alone and find out why you are attracted to a man like this. The bottom line is that unless he gets professional help and is able to change, your relationship is doomed. Next time, find a man who will be faithful to you.*

Booker sighed. One of the changes he'd wanted to make in the *Tribune* were these long answers to readers' questions, delivered by a nonprofessional. He'd called Adelaide Thomas and asked her to keep her responses short and witty, to save the counseling and analyzing for someone with the proper credentials. He'd thought he'd gotten through to her, but apparently his words had fallen on stubborn ears. He crossed out this and that, ending up with, *Dear Ain't Happy—I'd stop being home base while he plays the field!*

Booker stood to stretch his legs and was just in time to catch a glimpse of a familiar tumble of gold curls moving past his front window. By the time he got out on the sidewalk, Kristy was three doors farther along the block. He called her name and jogged to catch up with her.

"Hello," she said warmly, and suddenly fatigue fell away from Booker's shoulders like a discarded winter coat.

"Hello. Kind of chilly for an evening walk, isn't it?"

Kristy shrugged. She was encased in a candy-apple red wool cape, a scarf of blue and red draped casually over her shoulders. Booker thought she looked wonderful even though her eyes seemed sad. He took her arm and said, "May I walk you home?"

"Okay," she said, adding as they took their first step, "Don't you think you should close the newspaper door first?"

He looked over his shoulder. "Wait here—don't go away." He jogged back to the office and closed and locked the front door, leaving all the lights on. Well, he'd have to come back later, anyway, and finish working, so why not? He ran back to Kristy, ignoring the little voice that whispered in the back of his head. It was trying to say something about how he was acting like a schoolboy. He'd listen later.

"First newspaper is out day after tomorrow, right?" Kristy asked as they walked.

Booker, denying himself the pleasure of taking her hand mainly because he was afraid she'd snatch it back, said, "One o'clock sharp."

"Rudy Keeler was often late," Kristy said.

"Hm—" Booker said.

"But you won't be?"

"No."

"Why? What's the big deal?"

Booker looked at the woman beside him and wished she'd stop worrying about the newspaper. Couldn't she see the full moon in the clear sky, smell the sea, hear the distant bark of sea lions? He sighed and said, "We don't do our own printing. A press over in Pinecreek takes care of it for us, so we have to have the galleys ready to send over by eight-thirty in the morning if we want the paper by Wednesday. I'm not sure how Keeler managed to be late, but I won't."

Kristy nodded, then looked up at him and grinned. "I guess I've been properly put in my place."

"That wasn't my intention," he said. "I just wanted you to understand."

"Which I now do. Speaking of the paper, I hope you've decided not to mention Nancy's suicide."

Oh, great, he thought. He said, "It's news, isn't it?"

"I suppose so, but a lot of innocent people have been hurt by it. It doesn't make sense to me to hurt them further."

"How can a factual, discreet accounting of the incident end up further hurting people? Seems to me it would do just the opposite. It would clear the air, settle the gossip mongers."

"So you've heard the gossip, too?"

"Not really. I'm new in town, remember? But if you have, doesn't that prove my point?"

She glanced at him swiftly. "No. It's just feeding morbid curiosity."

"Kristy, Kristy. Let's not talk about this, okay? Just

wait. You'll find I'm not exploiting a young woman's misery, I promise.''

She nodded, her gaze once more directed toward the sidewalk. After a few minutes' silence—silence Booker used unsuccessfully to try to think of a neutral topic for conversation—she said, ''By the way, I got an audition mailer today for *Someday Soon*.''

''And which part are you trying out for?'' he asked.

''Anna Thorton, a sweet-tempered secretary, age about twenty. Think I can pass for twenty?''

''I would think you could pass for sixteen.''

''Thanks a lot.''

''This must be my own personal put-your-foot-in-your-mouth-day.''

''It's okay. I know you meant it as a compliment. I'm almost twenty-six years old, and I've looked exactly the same for ten years. I'll probably look like this until I'm sixty-five, when I'll lose my hair and my teeth in one fell swoop.''

Booker smiled.

After a moment Kristy said, ''You know, I thought at first after Nancy . . . died . . . that I'd sit this play out, but James Winterberg actually called everyone in *Tree Tops* and encouraged them to try out. He said we had to go on, that Nancy would have wanted it, that we'll dedicate this play to her. I think I'd like to be a part of that.''

''Sounds like you think a lot of Winterberg.''

''Of course. He's really quite special. And his wife and I have been friends for a long time.''

''The wispy-looking blonde?''

''Yes, Regina. How about you?'' she asked. ''Have

you changed your mind and decided to audition for a part?''

''Not me.''

She came to a halt outside a small house with two distinct entrances. ''The one on the left is mine. I'd ask you in, but it's late and I have school tomorrow . . . .''

Booker nodded. He yearned to pull her close, but she was already a step or two away. Was she purposely keeping her distance? Had the chatter all the way home been some kind of defense, and if so, against what? All she'd had to do was tell him she'd prefer to walk alone. He turned on his heels and began walking back toward Main Street. She called out her thanks, and he waved his hand briskly. Two could play this little game. It would be easier if he knew exactly what game they were playing, but of one thing he was certain: he wasn't jumping through hoops for anyone, man or woman.

Wednesday seemed to last forever. Kristy wasn't ready to admit she was anxious about the paper, but she was, and as soon as her last class left the room, she pulled her coat and purse from the closet behind her desk and made her way out of the school.

As she walked into town, she wondered why it mattered so much what Booker printed in his silly paper. No matter what was written, people would get over it in a day or so; by Friday the paper would be lining bird cages or stacked in recycling bins. Why did she care so much that Booker handle the matter in a way she found tasteful?

She parked the car in front of the newspaper office and deposited three dimes into the paper machine on the sidewalk. With some relief, she found the story in bold headlines at the top of the front page concerned the timber industry. She flipped the folded paper over and found another headline across the bottom of page one. This one chilled her to the bone.

Local Actress Plunges to Death, she read. She took a deep breath, which did nothing to quench the rage she felt rising up her throat, and made herself read on.

A young woman died late Saturday night on the jagged rocks below the balcony of prominent Cypress Hill businessman James Winterberg. According to Sheriff Norm Fuller, Nancy Collins, 24, was attending a party thrown by Winterberg for the cast and crew of his play, Tree Tops. Collins is thought to have died instantly upon impact. Sheriff Fuller said—

Kristy felt like shredding the paper. She read no further, but the black-and-white photo of the abandoned balcony loomed on the page as a gentle reminder of Saturday night. She folded the paper in half again and flung open the front door of the *Cypress Tribune.* She glared at the secretary until the trim, middle-aged woman glanced up and saw her. As the secretary stood, she said, "May I help you—"

Kristy interrupted. "You bet you can help me. I want to see Booker. Now!"

"I'm sorry," the secretary said, glancing nervously in the direction of a closed door. "He's in a meeting—"

"I don't care!" Kristy said. She strode behind the counter and tore open the door. She found Booker standing behind his desk. An elderly woman with a bun of improbable black hair stood facing him on the other side of the desk, her hand in the air between them as though she were scolding him. Both Booker and the woman froze in surprise at Kristy's abrupt entrance.

"I want to talk to you," Kristy said, her voice a low growl.

"You wait your turn, honey," the other woman said, coming back to life.

"This won't wait."

"Just get in line," the woman insisted. "This . . . this . . . man just ruined my column."

"Who cares about your column!" Kristy cried.

"Well . . . of all the nerve!" the woman sputtered.

Booker narrowed his eyes, but Kristy met his gaze without flinching. "Ruining a column is better than ruining lives," she said between clenched teeth. "Or don't you care about people's lives, Booker?"

Chapter Four

A few times in his life, A. W. Booker had wished he could evaporate off the face of the earth. Like the time his older brother found him necking with Kathy White, the older brother's girlfriend. Or the time in college when. . . . Well, never mind, those events were past history, and he'd lived through them no matter how uncomfortable it had been.

This was different. Two people who knew very little about newspapers were berating him for doing his job well. Adelaide he could handle—the woman was cranky but obviously in love with seeing her name in print. But Kristy. . . .

Had he really managed to put that look of distaste into her eyes? Why did he feel like crawling to her, circling her slender waist with his arms, begging her to forgive him? This was ridiculous! He had done nothing to be forgiven for. Nevertheless, he hated the pain he could detect under the anger, hated the fact that he was responsible for making her huge blue eyes swell with unshed tears.

These thoughts took place in the few seconds after Kristy accused Booker of being an unmitigated heel.

He looked directly at her and said, "Of course I care about people. I just don't happen to believe a factual reporting of an incident—"

"I bet you don't believe in anything!" she interrupted.

"I beg to differ," he said quietly.

It was a standoff, but Addie apparently saw it as an opportunity to get her point across for the seventh time. "You rewrote my answer to 'Ain't Happy.' You had no right—"

Booker turned to face the angry woman. "Of course I had a right. I'm your editor, remember? And we had talked about this, and you had promised."

"Rudy Keeler never changed a single word of my copy, not a single word. The man was a newspaper icon, and yet he saw fit to leave my answers alone."

Booker said, "I am not Rudy Keeler, Adelaide."

Addie narrowed her eyes. "No, you're not," she agreed at last. "You certainly are not. Well, that's it then. I quit."

Booker stared at her for a moment. At last he cleared his throat. "You what?"

"I quit. Unless you want to rethink your highhanded attitude, Mr. Booker, I quit. I will not allow my sensitive, thought-provoking answers to be ruined by an uncaring man! What do you know about people and their problems? What do you know about anything?"

This time Booker narrowed his eyes. "I imagine I know as much as you do," he said. "To my knowledge, you have no special training in counseling or a degree—"

"I am a woman!" she said imperiously.

"So what?" he answered in the same tone of voice.

Adelaide slapped her copy of the *Cypress Tribune* down on his desk. "Then you write the column, Mr. High and Mighty. You'll be begging me to come back within a month. I quit." With this, she turned on her heels, tore open the outer door, and slammed it behind her.

Booker sighed. He looked back at Kristy and said, "Your turn."

She shook her head, looking more resigned now than angry. "What's the use?" she asked. "It's done. I had hoped you'd spare the Winterberg and the Collins families, but you didn't. I have no right to be disappointed in you. I barely know you. I had just hoped . . . well, at first I thought. . . . Oh, never mind!"

She left quietly, the impact of her disappointed words a hundred times more immobilizing than Addie's tirade had been. Booker sat down slowly, his brow furrowed, and wished he didn't care one way or the other what Kristy Wilder thought.

Kristy passed the next couple of days in a mild depression. She wasn't sure exactly why she was depressed, wasn't even sure she wanted to know. It was enough to know it would pass if she gave herself time. Relief came in an unexpected form when the box from the television shopping channel finally came. This time her mother had chosen for her a giant cubic zirconia ring set in real gold. Kristy put the ring on and laughed out loud. It looked genuine enough, but heavenly days, where did Mom think she went in little old Cypress Hill that she could wear fur coats and diamonds, even if they were fake? Kristy put the ring back in the box, still chuckling.

She was walking home from school two days after the paper hit the stands when she ran into Regina Winterberg coming out of a stationery store. Kristy stopped to talk and knew immediately her mild bout of depression had been nothing next to Regina's current state.

"How are you feeling?" she asked, concern for Regina making her blunt.

Regina brushed a few stray hairs off her high forehead. "I'm okay," she said without conviction.

Kristy nodded, biting her lip. She said, "Well, you look great! What did James say when you told him—"

"I haven't yet," Regina interrupted. "And you promised you wouldn't, Kristy, remember?"

"I won't, but really, Regina—"

"You know how James is during a play. Nothing exists for him, not me or the furniture stores, nothing but the play. I intend to wait until that's over and I have his undivided attention."

"I see," Kristy said.

Regina opened the sack she had in one hand and took out a copy of the *Cypress Tribune*. "Did you see this?" she asked.

Kristy nodded.

"I didn't think they made such a big deal out of suicides," Regina said bitterly.

"It doesn't really mention the word suicide," Kristy pointed out. "It just says she fell to her death and that no foul play was suspected."

"But everyone knows," Regina said. "James is

livid! He said for two cents he'd rip Booker's head off.''

"Booker is a newspaperman," Kristy said gently.

Regina shook her head. "Why are you defending him?"

"I'm not!" Kristy protested.

"Yes, you are. Honestly, Kristy, I thought you were our friend.''

"I am your friend," Kristy said. "Please, Regina, calm down. It can't be good for you to be so upset . . . now. In your condition, I mean.''

Regina stuffed the paper back into the sack with shaking hands. "I know, I know."

"Have you been to see a doctor?"

Regina shrugged.

"Make an appointment," Kristy begged.

Regina squared her thin shoulders. "I thought you said I looked great."

Kristy put her hand on Regina's arm. "You do. You're beautiful, and you know it, you compliment hound. But you've been under a strain.''

Regina sighed. "Yes, you're right. But I don't need a doctor. Please, don't worry about me." She walked away, her shoulders squared, every inch a strong but troubled woman. Kristy's heart went out to her, and despite Regina's directions, she couldn't help but be worried about her.

Actually, she had two worries. Number one: What was wrong with Regina? Why was she so jumpy? Why had her face drained of color when Kristy first spoke her name? Why was she pale and visibly thinner in just a week? Kristy knew she couldn't tell James about

Regina's pregnancy, but shouldn't she ask him to make sure Regina saw a doctor? Would that be prying busybody work or the act of a concerned friend?

Number two worry: Had she really defended Booker? She tried to mentally review her conversation with Regina. No, she couldn't have excused his article, could she have? Impossible. She'd think about this one later.

By the time Kristy got home, she'd made up her mind. Let Regina be angry with her; a good friend doesn't turn their back on someone when they're in need of help even if they don't know they need the help. She would approach her concern for Regina's health in a roundabout fashion so as not to frighten James or break her promise to Regina, but she would call him. Before she could lose her courage, she picked up the phone and called the Winterberg house, hoping Regina hadn't had time to drive all the way home yet.

James answered the phone with a curt, ''Yes?''

''James, I'm glad it's you. This is Kristy Wilder calling.''

''Kristy, what a pleasure to hear your voice. What can I do for you?''

''I'd like to talk to you about the other night, James, the night Nancy Collins killed herself. It was terribly upsetting to Regina.''

He was silent for a moment; then he said, ''May I call you back, Kristy? I have a few people here right now.''

''Of course. I didn't mean to interfere.''

"That's quite all right. I'll get back to you later this evening."

"Fine." It wasn't until Kristy hung up that she remembered tonight was the night she had to be at the school for parent-teacher night. Well, no matter. Auditions were tomorrow afternoon—she'd talk to him afterward.

It was the first time most of the actors had been back to the theater since Nancy died, Kristy realized, and it was as though her presence haunted the empty stage. Even James seemed to feel it. The only person who looked comfortable was Regina Winterberg, who was seated between her husband and costume designer Hank Roscoe, who liked being in on each production from the beginning. Two crochet hooks were doing battle with each other in Regina's hands. Kristy could hardly believe the woman in the audience was the same one she'd seen and talked to the day before. At least she wouldn't have to talk to James now. Regina had obviously come to terms with Nancy's death and decided to go on with her life. Kristy found herself staring at James, smiling when he caught her looking, thinking Regina must have confided her pregnancy to her husband.

Kristy had read the play the night before and had been mildly disappointed. She knew Lydia was rejected in the end by Fenton Bywater, but she hadn't expected it to all end so stoically. Where was the biting punch of *Tree Tops*, the heart-wrenching twist that left the audiences' hearts in their mouths? Well, it wasn't hers to question; the part of Anna Thorton, secretary to Lydia Honeydew, was perfect.

Kristy was nervous, which was preferable to the way she'd been feeling since the afternoon she stormed into Booker's office, intending to tell him off. She'd tried not to think about Booker much the last few days, and indeed, Regina's troubles had distracted her for a while. But he seemed to hover on the edge of her thoughts, always present, always too far to reach. It was infuriating to think so much about a man she didn't even like.

Kristy's thoughts were interrupted when Summer Sanders gently poked her in the ribs. "They called your name twice," Summer said. "Wake up."

"What? Oh, thanks, Summer." Kristy stepped forward into the ring of light center stage. She glanced toward Summer, who gave her a thumbs-up sign.

As Kristy performed the piece she'd prepared for the audition, she forgot all about Booker and James and even Nancy Collins. When she was finished, she heard soft applause from Summer's direction and the mostly empty audience section.

"Very nice," James said.

Kristy said, "Thank you."

"It says on your audition form you would like the part of Anna Thorton?"

"That's right," Kristy said.

James smiled broadly and nodded. Kristy knew he wouldn't commit himself until the auditions were over, but she felt fairly confident the role was hers. It seemed Summer agreed, for when Kristy returned to the sidelines, Summer smiled warmly. "I'm sure you got the part," she said.

"I hope so. Now who's not paying attention? They just called your name," Kristy teased.

Summer walked gracefully to center stage and proceeded to wow everyone in the theater with a powerful performance in which emotions traveled across her lovely face at breakneck speeds and words danced off her tongue with profound ease. The applause this time wasn't lightweight.

"Wonderful!" James yelled, spontaneously rising to his feet when she finished. He rushed onto the stage and took Summer's hands into his. "You were spectacular, my dear, just spectacular."

The only people who seemed a little put out over Summer's obvious talent and potential to carry a leading-lady role were the Barnetts, who smiled with their mouths and frowned with their eyes.

After a few minutes the hoopla died down and the stage manager called out the last name, "A. W. Booker."

Kristy twirled around and came face to face with Booker, who winked at her. She frowned at him and looked away, but not before her heart caught at the sight of him. What was he doing here?

Booker took his place and recited a small part from a popular play. When he finished, James said, "Thank you, Mr. Booker." His voice was controlled and a tad cold, and Kristy thought of what Regina had said about James wanting to rip Booker's handsome head off his broad shoulders. Of course, Regina hadn't said it quite that way. . . .

Booker nodded. He walked to the opposite side of the stage. When Kristy dared a quick glance in his direction, she found him staring at her, his expression unfathomable. She looked away.

James came back on stage, his hands full of notepads and the forms the prospective actors had filled out. Regina stayed in the audience, her fingers busily wielding crochet hooks. Again Kristy found herself thinking Regina must have changed her mind and confided her good news to James.

"Well, now," James said. "As you know, there aren't that many parts, and since you've all auditioned, I may as well tell you what I've decided here and now."

Just then, Jack, the stage manager, showed up with a white envelope which he slipped to James. "Messenger brought it, said you should read it right away," he said in a stage whisper.

"What messenger?" James snapped as he took the envelope.

"Some kid. He's already long gone."

Obviously annoyed, James opened the envelope and withdrew a folded sheet of white paper. As he read, he turned his back to the small gathering. When he looked up and turned back around, he looked bewildered, and his eyes moved from face to face as though he were in a trance. The last person he looked at was Kristy, and the look in his eyes was enough to freeze water.

"What is it?" Regina called from the audience.

As he looked at his wife, he refolded the paper and stuck it in the envelope, then put both of them into his pocket. "Nothing," he said, his voice wooden.

"James?"

"Nothing," he repeated sternly, his gaze once again resting on Kristy. He seemed to be struggling with a compulsion to stare at her, a compulsion Kristy didn't understand. At last he cleared his throat and said, "Here are the parts. The leading male role of Fenton Bywater will be played by Todd Andrews. Leading lady Lydia Honeydew will be played by Kristy Wilder."

"Me?" Kristy blurted out.

James looked at her with cold gray eyes. "Yes, Kristy, you."

"But Summer—"

"Will play the part of Anna Thorton."

As James assigned the rest of the parts, Kristy looked at Summer, who regarded her with a look of baffled bewilderment Kristy knew mirrored her own expression. "I don't understand," she whispered to Summer.

Summer managed to smile. "Congratulations," she said.

"But, Summer—"

"Don't, Kristy. The decision has been made. Don't humiliate me by questioning it again, please."

Kristy bit her lip. She glanced across the small circle and found Booker staring at her. He smiled and Kristy felt like throwing her arms around his solid-looking neck. She left the stage and began walking home.

It wasn't that she didn't want a leading part—someday. Someday when she was ready for it, when someone more deserving didn't get pushed aside. Why in the world had she been chosen? It made absolutely no sense at all. She knew she shouldn't have left and half hoped James would be angry enough with her to take away the lead. All she'd wanted was the role of Anna Thorton. Twenty-nine lines, on stage almost all the time but never in the limelight. That's what she'd wanted, not this!

"Wait up!" The voice came from behind her, and Kristy stopped walking and waited until the man who had called out to her caught up.

"Don't you ever drive anywhere?" Booker asked as he came to a stop beside her. She'd seen him run at least a block, and yet his breathing wasn't labored.

"Not often," Kristy said. She looked at him and added, "What do you want, Booker?"

"I just want to talk to you," he said softly, his gaze directed at the sidewalk.

"We talked a few days ago," she said. "I don't think we have anything left to say." She began walking again. She wasn't surprised when he fell into step beside her.

"Put our differences about what constitutes news aside for a moment. What about today?"

"What about today?" Kristy snapped. She was at her duplex door by now. She opened the lock and stepped inside.

"Let me come in," he said.

"I'm tired, and like I said—"

"Remember the first night we met? It was at a crowded party before all the crazy things began to happen, remember?"

"Of course," Kristy said.

"We went outside and talked. The night wind ruffled your hair and your skirt. We flirted. If those egomaniacal Barnetts hadn't forced everyone into the room to hear them decimate *The Sound of Music* and Nancy Collins hadn't chosen that night to leap to her death, we would have spent the whole night out there. Eventually you would have been as overwhelmed with my masculine charms as I was with your feminine ones. We might have kissed. We might have made a date for a movie or a walk on the beach.''

"Where is all this going?'' Kristy asked.

"You liked the man you met that night, I know you did. Well, here he is on your doorstep, and all he wants is to come inside and be your friend.''

"That's all he wants?''

He smiled. "No. But let him in, anyway.''

Kristy held the door aside, and he went into the living room ahead of her. She closed the door and saw him looking over her living space. She knew all he would see was a modest one bedroom house which was tastefully if not elaborately decorated in muted greens and yellows, the glass tables echoing the floor-to-ceiling window panels which occupied the southern wall. The only bright note of unsubdued color was a poster for *Tree Tops*.

"This is very nice,'' Booker said.

"Thank you. Would you like something hot to drink?''

"Coffee if you have it.''

"I can make it. I think I'll have something stronger.''

"You're really upset about this play, aren't you?''

"I'm embarrassed,'' Kristy said. "I'm mortified. I'm going to quit the play, that's all there is to it.''

She sat down on the edge of the sofa and clasped her hands together, completely forgetting about making coffee or finding herself something strong and stiff to deaden her feelings.

"I don't know what happened to James," she said. "Do you know how the audition sheet described the character of Lydia? 'A hauntingly beautiful woman, as tall and dark as Fenton, her would-be lover, age thirty.' That's an exact quote. It also perfectly describes Summer Sanders. Oh, this is insane!"

Booker sat down next to her, his solid weight dipping the delicate sofa. He put his hand on her knee and said, "I agree."

She turned to face him and found his mouth dangerously close. She blinked rapidly, appalled to feel tears gathering in the corners of her eyes. "You do?" she said at last.

"I do. It was obvious to everyone that until he got the mysterious note, he was about to give Summer the larger role. Something in the note made him change his mind."

Kristy nodded. "But what?"

"Either something about Summer—"

"No. She's . . . she's a darling."

"Or something about you."

"Me?"

"Do you have any other ideas? And another strange thing. Why did he give me a part? He hates my guts, but he signed me on as Ken, the dull-witted gardener."

"I remember the description for that part, too," Kristy said. " 'A handsome, if not bright, gardener madly in love with Lydia.' " He was certainly handsome, she mused silently. All his talk of remembering their short time together before Nancy jumped off that balcony had reminded her how fascinating he was as well. And afterward he'd been brave and competent, protective and kind. Had she been unfair to him about the newspaper? What would she have done with the story if she owned the paper and it was her first edition in a new place?

"I have a penny here," he said softly, "to spend on a thought or two."

The day was fading, and late sunlight slanted in through the dining-room shutters, creating a striped pattern on the living-room rug. The room was dark and warm, and Kristy felt Booker's hand lift from her knee and touch her face. She leaned into his touch, greedy for the feel of him. His fingers ran over the top of her lips, and she looked up into those deep-brown eyes and felt consumed. He leaned forward until his lips were so close she could feel their magnetism. Then he pulled away and laughed softly to himself.

"What are you laughing about?" she asked.

"Us. Our timing is rotten, isn't it?"

"What do you mean?"

"You're very upset about this play. Until ten minutes ago you were very upset with me. This isn't the time to start something." He swore softly under his breath and added, "I can hardly believe I'm saying all this instead of kissing you."

"Neither can I," Kristy said, but then she sighed and sat up straight. "On the other hand, you do have a point."

"How about going to get something to eat?" he said.

Kristy, intending to say no, said, "Okay."

They ended up at the Lonesome Tortoise, side by side at a wooden plank table pushed up close to a wall. Kristy wondered if Booker sat down next to her rather than across from her because of the noise level or because he wanted to stay close. He seemed to answer her unspoken question when he leaned down and said, "The only way we're going to be able to talk is to shout into each other's ears. Romantic, isn't it?"

Kristy smiled at him. It was safe, anyway.

"This place is . . . different," Booker said.

The single large room was crowded and dim and filled with a thin, hazy layer of smoke. Hanging on the rough planks which constituted the walls were old tortoise shells, fishing nets and floats, framed photographs of smiling people, and painfully amateurish paintings such as the one of a tortoise playing poker with a rabbit and a monkey which hung over Booker and Kristy's table.

A long bar ran across the right wall of the room with battered stools, each occupied by a Cypress Hill resident seemingly intent on enjoying a Saturday night on the town. More crowded tables were lined up in the middle of the room along with a pool table or two and a lot of people standing in groups, talking. Loud country-western music blared from the jukebox. The beverage of choice appeared to be beer, by the mug or the pitcher, straight from the taps of exposed barrels of ale.

"What's good to eat here?" Booker asked Kristy, leaning close again. The feel of his arm pressed against hers, and his breath caressing her ear made Kristy wonder if this was going to be any easier than staying at her place would have been.

"Order the New York steak and onion rings," she said, turning to face him. That put them nose to nose, and they both looked away at once.

They ordered dinner and accepted huge chilled mugs of draft beer. Booker put his head very close to Kristy's head so that he didn't have to shout so loud and said, "Maybe we're reading something into nothing."

Was he talking about their awareness of each other? She was about to say, "Speak for yourself, buddy," when he continued.

"I mean, I heard your audition. I thought you were great."

Oh, the play. "Did you really?" she asked, a little distracted by the nearness of his perfect lips to her eyes.

"Yes. Maybe Winterberg decided on the spot to change his conception of Lydia. Maybe he saw you and decided you were the right woman to play the part."

Kristy thought about this. She wanted to believe this train of thought. "I thought you were good, too," she said. "I'm glad you decided to audition."

"So maybe we both just convinced Winterberg we were perfect for the parts he gave us because of our acting ability."

"Do you really believe that?" Kristy asked.

Before he could answer, the jukebox went dead.

They looked up and found a low stage at the far right corner had been brightly lit, and a man wearing a cowboy hat was standing at a microphone in the middle of it. Several other men with guitars, fiddles, and drums formed an arc in back of him.

"Ladies and gents," he said. He had to say it twice as the first time was practically drowned in the noise a crowd makes right before it decides to be quiet. " . . . the fellow who needs no introductions but is getting one, anyway," the man continued. "You all know him and love him, and we're just mighty happy he's agreed to come back and sing for us here at the Lonesome Tortoise. I give you Charlie Hook!" He waved his hat, stepping off the stage as Charlie Hook stepped on.

Kristy and Booker turned to face each other as thunderous applause shook the small restaurant/bar. "I'd forgotten about him," Kristy said.

"Me, too," Booker said.

The band started playing a familiar melody Kristy couldn't name as Charlie spoke into the microphone.

"I want to dedicate this song to the prettiest little gal I ever knew," he said softly. "Hair like spun gold, eyes the color of the sky. I miss you, Nancy. This one is for you."

Charlie Hook had sung no more than a word or two when a man at the bar stood up. "You don't go singing to Nancy," he shouted. "You have no right to sing to her. She was my girl—mine, you hear!"

Everyone heard. While the band continued playing, Charlie Hook stopped singing and stared at the slender man with the black leather jacket who was weaving his way toward the stage. Eventually the music stopped, and except for a few nervous coughs, the room was strangely silent.

"Who in the world is that?" Booker asked. "Could it possibly be the illusive Tom?"

"No, it's Jim Turner," Kristy said. "Nancy broke up with him a few weeks before she died. He looks awful."

"He's drunk," Booker said. "Maybe I should stop him."

Kristy pointed. "Look."

The man who had introduced Charlie Hook was making his way through the crowd to intercept Jim Turner's path, but the young man was too slippery for him. He made it all the way to the stage.

"Did you hear me?" he shouted at Charlie. "Nancy was mine. Come down here and fight like a man."

Kristy watched Charlie Hook. He was twice as big as Jim and twice as sober. He stepped down from the low stage and caught Jim in his big hands right as Jim put his weight into a punch. The punch landed nowhere. Jim dissolved into a sobbing heap. By then a couple of his friends had made it to the stage area. One on each side, they took Jim from Charlie Hook and, supporting him, began making their way back through the crowd which carefully parted before them. The bartender handed one of the men Jim's hat; then all three of them left the Lonesome Tortoise.

Charlie Hook stepped back onto the stage. "Like I said," he repeated, his voice choking, "this song is for little Nancy."

Chapter Five

The morning sun was bright, a spring rarity Booker enjoyed. He rolled over in his sleeping bag and squinted his eyes against the rays streaming in the curtainless windows. He was sleeping on the floor in the vast living room whose sole furnishing was an oak chest he'd bought at an antique store on his way north. All the rest of his furniture was in transit, but even when it finally arrived, he knew it would barely begin to fill the corners of this huge house he'd bought mainly on impulse.

He sat up and gazed out the window at the view which had inspired this impulsive buy: trees. As far as the eye could see, trees. Big old shaggy redwoods, graceful alder budding an innocent green, Pacific madrone with shiny red bark, an occasional fir, pine, coastal oak. All the trees were his.

Ten years he'd lived in L.A. Ten years he'd stared out his apartment window at other apartment buildings. Ten years he'd dreamed about trees, of all things; little ones, big ones, the kind that lose their leaves and the kind that stay green all the time. Deciduous and evergreen, he remembered, and smiled at his trees.

76

Oh, but the house, he thought as he looked around the barren room. There were twelve more rooms, including three bathrooms. Thirteen rooms compared to four in the apartment. Thirteen rooms to furnish and clean and look into once in a while. The ugly fact was he was going to have to break down and go furniture shopping; only thing was, he wasn't too fond of brand-new furniture. Made a place look like something out of a magazine, not a house a man lived in.

This was the kind of a house to raise a family in, he thought idly as he rolled up his sleeping bag and was immediately startled. A family! Not once in his thirty-two years had he ever considered himself the kind of man to have children. It was all Kristy's fault.

Thinking of her woke him completely. He couldn't remember a time in his life when he'd felt this way about a woman. Even his ex-wife hadn't touched his heart the way Kristy did.

What a mistake Catherine, the ex, had been! They'd both been young, but he'd promised to love her for life, and he'd been willing to make every effort to do so. Catherine, on the other hand, got tired of struggling with finances, got tired of his unpredictable and sometimes long hours, ultimately got tired of him. She'd run off seven years ago, long before his investment in the satellite TV log paid off, long before he had enough money to finally fulfill his dream of living and working in a small town, owning a paper, making a difference. It didn't matter—she would have hated it here. He knew she was remarried to an investment banker in New York. Good for Catherine. Good for the investment banker, and especially good for A. W. Booker.

After a shower—he did have towels—he made a cup of instant coffee and looked at the telephone. With a smile on his lips, he picked up the receiver and put it down again. He longed to call Kristy, but something made him hesitate.

The night before had been a strange one even before the near fight between Charlie Hook and Jim Turner. It had physically hurt not to kiss Kristy. To be that close to feeling her in his arms, and then turning away from it because he'd sensed she'd regret whatever they shared as soon as a new day dawned, had been an unbearable act of bravery on his part. She'd never know what his self-control had cost him!

He stared at the phone as he leafed absently through his paper, wondering what he could do on this beautiful Sunday that didn't involve working. Thanks to Adelaide Thomas's mutiny, he had the Ask Addie column to write, but that shouldn't take long, and he hated the thought of burying himself inside the office. Surely something was happening outside that he and Kristy could do together. Something that wasn't intimate or threatening. Something which would allow them to chat and get to know each other, though in his heart he felt as though he'd known her forever. The classified ads caught his eye, and suddenly he knew exactly what to do.

Kristy hooked a gold chain around her neck, deciding the precious metal looked good against the pink of her sweater. She was glad Booker had called, though he would have been the last person on earth she would have suspected liked rummaging around in yard sales.

She heard a knock on the front door and grabbed a coat and her purse. She had no idea where Booker lived, but it had taken him less than half an hour to get to her door.

They started at one end of town and ended up at the other, following the ads placed in Booker's newspaper. Kristy knew all the addresses and most of the people running the sales. By the time they got to the north end of town, the back of Booker's pickup was loaded with four mahogany chairs, two oak dressers, an oak filing cabinet, and a battered old antique roll-top desk. Booker had confessed he enjoyed refinishing furniture; Kristy thought his purchases today would keep him busy for months.

It was almost four in the afternoon before he pulled up outside the Collins house. A big For Sale sign was pounded into the front yard, which looked newly mowed. In fact, the whole house looked as though it had received a quick face lift; Kristy thought Anne Argot, Ida's sister, must have been hard at work the last few days.

"Nancy Collins's house?" Booker asked. "Her mother is moving already?"

"The rumors about Nancy's death are hard on her," Kristy said. "She has a twin sister who wants to take her back to Spokane, Washington and get her away from here."

"She won't want to sell her old furniture to me," Booker said softly.

Kristy silently agreed. "We won't tell her who you are," she said.

"Yes, we will. Maybe she'll be levelheaded."

"Hm—"

The yard was still cluttered with miscellaneous items, and a sign tacked onto the porch railing announced much more could be found inside the house. Since the other sales had been picked over by Sunday afternoon, Kristy was surprised. She supposed it was people's reluctance to face Ida Collins.

Anne came out onto the porch. Her lined face broke into a warm smile when she saw Kristy. "Did you come for Sis's sale?" she asked.

"My friend did. It doesn't look as though you've had much of a turnout."

"Funny little town you have here. Full of rumors and secret glances. I can't wait to get Ida out of it."

"Isn't this move a little sudden?" Kristy asked. "I know it's none of my business, but I'm concerned about her."

"I know, I know, but it was her idea to do it this fast." Anne looked directly at Booker and added, "Now then, mister, what kind of things are you looking for?"

Kristy glanced up and saw Ida Collins on the porch, watching. She smiled at the older woman, who seemed to do her best to conjure up a smile but wasn't quite able to pull it off. Huge dark circles ringed her eyes, and the bones in her face seemed to be dangerously close to her skin. Anne was right—Ida did need to leave Cypress Hill.

Booker said, "Just about anything. But in all fairness, I suppose I should tell you who I am. I'm the man who bought out old man Keeler. I'm the new owner/publisher of the *Cypress Tribune*."

Ida Collins gasped, her hand flying to cover her mouth. Kristy took a few steps up onto the porch, readying herself to be kicked off. Below her, Booker said, "I can't tell you how sorry I am, Mrs. Collins, about your loss. I only met Nancy once. She was a very beautiful woman."

Ida's hand slipped down to fidget with her other hand in front of her. She said, "Thank you. Mr. Booker, isn't it?"

"That's right."

"Well, thank you. Yes, she was pretty. Every time I look at this girl," and she nodded at Kristy, "I'm reminded of her, they look that much alike. And you're one of the few people in this town who have had the decency to express their sorrow to me face to face, and you don't even know me. I read what you wrote in the paper, too. I was glad you didn't actually say Nancy killed herself because, Mr. Booker, I don't care what anyone says, I will never believe she did."

Kristy let out a long breath. Ida disappeared back into the house, and Booker and Anne followed. Kristy sat on the steps, her eyes closed against the glare of the sun. Her sweater was too hot, but the heat felt good. She thought about Ida's composed reaction and the night before when Charlie Hooks had grabbed Jim Turner's shoulders almost gently while the drunk man tried to hit him. People were full of surprises.

"I'll send a truck for everything tomorrow," she heard Booker say as he came out onto the porch. Kristy stood and brushed off her jeans. Ida was holding Nancy's briefcase and a check. She pocketed the check and then walked down the steps to Kristy.

"I know you and Nancy weren't close friends," she said awkwardly. "My Nancy didn't have many friends, not female ones, anyway. But she did care for you more than she maybe let on, and I thought that you being a teacher and all, you might be able to use her briefcase."

Kristy took the case. "I . . . I don't know what to say—"

"Don't say anything. I was real upset the night you came to return this, or I would have told you then to keep it. I don't know where she got it or even when. I looked through it a little. There's just some papers in it, things having to do with that play *Tree Tops* you and she were in. Throw them away, whatever you want."

Kristy let the case fall by her side. "Thank you," she said. "I'll think of you and Nancy everytime I use this."

Ida nodded, her dark eyes bright.

Booker joined them. "Mrs. Collins, did Nancy ever mention a man by the name of Tom?"

As she slowly shook her head, her gaze changed from curious to indifferent. "Sheriff asked me the same thing. I'll tell you what I told him. As far as I know, Nancy was crazy about a cowboy singer named Charlie Hook. I told her he was too old for her, but Nancy never did listen to me much."

Booker nodded. "Well, thanks again for all the lovely furniture. I'll give everything a good home."

"You can burn it for firewood for all I care," Ida said firmly. "This stuff belongs to the past, and it's over. I'm leaving Cypress Hill, and I'm going to try not to look back." With a final nod she climbed the stairs and disappeared into the house.

Sitting on the wooden chairs pulled up to the kitchen counter in Booker's house, Kristy and Booker ate cereal for dinner. "Not quite as good as last night's steaks," he said, "but the company is just as good."

"At least it's quieter," Kristy said. "Did you really buy every piece of Ida Collins's furniture?"

"Every stick. Not all of it is really good, but a few pieces are. I'll take what I can use and give the rest to charity. Ida Collins was just so anxious. . . . "

His voice trailed off. Kristy, touched by his generosity, looked around the huge house. "You're still going to need more," she said.

He shrugged. "I'll save that for someday."

"Someday?"

Did he actually blush? "Someday," he repeated. "You know, when I marry and have a wife to help me."

Kristy smiled. "You never struck me as the marrying kind, Booker. What do your initials, A.W., stand for?"

"How'd you know my initials?"

"They called them out yesterday at the audition."

"It's none of your business," he said, a smile taking any sting out of his words.

"Another 'someday' thing?"

"Maybe. Listen, we didn't talk about last night. What did you make out of Jim Turner tackling Charlie Hook?"

"I know you're evading my question, but now that you bring it up, I have to admit I was stunned. Mainly by how compassionate Charlie Hook seemed. Both of those men really cared for Nancy."

"Imagine the shape the mysterious Tom must be in."

"I wonder who he is," Kristy mused. "It was so unlike Nancy to keep a boyfriend a secret. You know, I thought I knew about everyone in town, but I just can't think of a Tom or Thomas. Not that it really matters. I'm just curious."

"You'd make a good reporter," Booker said, pouring more milk on his third bowl of corn flakes.

"Wait a second. There are a couple of guys named Tom in town. It's just so preposterous to think of either one of them with Nancy that I didn't think of them before. One is Tom Jones. He's a married fisherman I heard about through a friend who buys tuna off his boat every summer. The other one is Tom Savage."

"What does Tom Savage do?"

"Tom Savage is young. Very young. I had him in my class a couple of years ago. Right now, I think he's got a job at the computer store selling software."

"They don't seem likely."

"Still, if it was one of them, maybe they'd admit to it and that would explain Nancy's despondency. I mean, one is a married man, and the other is five years younger than she was, so if it was either one of them, it would explain why she didn't tell us all about him."

"Maybe it was Charlie Hook and she didn't mention his name because she didn't want to. Her mother was set against him, remember?"

"Then why did Nancy say, 'Tom is lost to me now; there's no reason to go on,' or words to that effect?"

"I don't know."

"Listen, if it is either one of our local Toms and he'll admit to it, maybe he'll tell me what happened between him and Nancy and I can tell Ida Collins and she can begin to accept her daughter's suicide because like it or not, Booker, two dozen people heard Nancy's last words, and one poor soul watched her fling herself into space."

"You want a job on the newspaper?"

"What? Oh, you tease!"

He crunched his way through another bite of cereal, swallowed, and said, "I think I know how you feel about Ida Collins. She looks like she's walking the edge of control right now, as though any little nudge could push her off into a breakdown."

Kristy nodded; then she glanced at her watch. "When you're finished eating, I'd better get on home. School tomorrow, and rehearsal tomorrow night." At the thought of the rehearsal, Kristy's spirits sank. She'd have to face James Winterberg and Summer Sanders. She squared her shoulders and ignored the acid dripping into her stomach. She'd concentrate on helping Ida and leave the rest to work itself out.

"I thought you'd insist on walking home," he said with a deep twinkle in his eyes.

"Not on your life," she told him. "You live six miles out of town. I'm not in that good shape."

Booker let his eyes roam slowly up Kristy's legs and body, ending at her face. "Could have fooled me," he said in a way that made Kristy's heart race.

"Just finish eating," she said.

* * *

In her dreams, James Winterberg clapped Kristy on her shoulders, handed her a script with the name Anna Thorton underlined in red ink, and said, "It was just a joke, Kristy. Of course Summer is playing Lydia." Then everyone laughed, and Kristy felt a wave of relief wash over her. Just a joke.

It didn't work out that way. She arrived early, intending on talking to James before everyone else arrived. Henry Sanders, the house manager and Summer's grandfather, let Kristy in the stage door, but he barely returned her greeting and refused to meet her eyes. Kristy was so embarrassed, she wanted to run away.

She went backstage instead and found James deep in conversation with Len Waters, the set designer.

Both men looked up at the sound of Kristy's footsteps. Len was about thirty. His skin was pale, but his eyes were like two bright-blue gemstones. He was tall and lanky, his long fingers tapered and artistic looking. Thanks to Len, the sets always looked vibrant and better than anything in real life ever could.

Len smiled at Kristy, but there was either a missing degree of warmth or Kristy was becoming paranoid. "I'm sorry to interrupt," Kristy said. "James, I need to talk to you."

Len cleared his throat. "I'll go check the inventory to see if we have the necessary lumber for this set," he said as he left.

James turned his gaze to Kristy. She felt like a fresh lettuce leaf thrust beneath hot water: limp. Screwing up her courage, she said, "I need to talk to you about my part."

"Like you needed to talk to me before the auditions?" he asked, his voice low.

"What?"

"You called me, remember?"

Kristy nodded. "Oh, that. Well, like I told you, I wanted to talk to you about Regina."

"About Regina," he said, his voice sounding skeptical. "You never did *talk* to me about Regina, though, did you?"

"It didn't seem to be necessary, after all," Kristy said, remembering the look of contentment on Regina's face the very next day as she sat in the almost empty theater during auditions, her hands expertly wielding the crochet hooks.

James laughed. "What a little master of understatement you are!" he said. "Now listen to me. You have the role of Lydia, and as your director I will talk to you in that capacity. But I don't expect to talk to you beyond the play. Am I making myself clear?"

Kristy felt her jaw drop. "I don't understand—"

"What's to understand? I gave you the role of Lydia. I expect you to perform the role adequately and not make a fool out of me. Is that too much to ask?"

"Of course not—"

"Good."

Kristy had no idea what lay behind the outpouring of venom she could practically see coming out of James's eyes. The only thing she could think of was that he'd told Regina that Kristy had called to talk about her. Had Regina assumed the call meant Kristy was going to tell him about her pregnancy? If so, Regina would view this as a double-cross and be furious. Had she then finally told James the big news, and was her fury with Kristy's supposed interference influencing James's behavior?

Kristy longed to explain. She felt like the kids she taught who sometimes became deeply entangled in various social situations with their peers. How many times had she heard them tell each other, "He said this," and "I meant that?" Somethimes it seemed almost impossible to untangle things and discover the truth.

There was another possibility, Kristy realized. Had Regina told James that Kristy defended Booker's newspaper? Could he possibly be angry about that? If he was worried about his public image, perhaps. But why would he cast her in a leading role, and why give Booker a role at all?

"James," she said, but was interrupted by voices which signaled the arrival of the rest of the cast.

As James walked past her, he said, "Didn't you want the role of Lydia?"

"Well, no."

That halted him. "You didn't?" he snapped.

Kristy drove deep into her soul and came up with a piece of honesty that surprised even her. "Well, of course I dreamed of it, but—"

He laughed. "And you found a way to make your dreams come true, didn't you?"

Did that mean he recognized how hard she'd worked on the audition piece? If so, why was he upset? "I guess I did," she told him, and on the spot decided to play the hand dealt her and to stop apologizing about her part. "I'm glad you understand," she told James, a hint of defiance in her voice.

"Oh, I understand, all right," he said, and with his casual grace walked away toward the rest of the cast.

They read through the play. Summer made Anna Thorton sound wonderful. Kristy hoped her voice didn't sound as wooden as she felt as she exchanged empty words with her co-star, Todd Andrews, words which would have to evolve into smoldering banter before opening night. Summer's attitude toward Kristy was so natural and kind that pretty soon everyone else followed suit, and the tension Kristy had felt seemed to disappear.

Booker mumbled his lines, which earned him a quick frown from James, a frown Booker didn't seem to notice. All and all, Kristy was happy when the rehearsal was over and they were all told to come back the next night.

"I have to get to the newspaper office and work on the Ask Addie column," Booker said as he shrugged on a leather jacket.

"I'll see you tomorrow night," Kristy told him.

The second issue of the *Cypress Tribune* didn't create a single ripple in the small town of Cypress Hill. The Ask Addie column wasn't quite as easy to write as Booker had assumed it would be; for one thing, there were dozens of letters written to the newspaper with Ask Addie written on the envelopes, letters he would have forwarded if Adelaide Thomas hadn't quit. As it was, he'd had to plow his way through letters ranging from "In Love With My Son's Wife," to "Help! My Sixteen-Year-Old Boyfriend Is Really

Thirty,'' settling on two for the column. He made his
answers as snappy and tart as he could, figuring a
nonprofessional should shy away from sounding too
official. Not that that had ever worried Adelaide
Thomas!

As the week passed, Booker was pleased to see the
cast and crew at the theater treating Kristy like he
assumed they always had in the past. He realized this
was largely due to the natural way Summer Sanders
acted, and he was grateful, which was a funny way to
feel. Kristy wasn't his to worry about—he hadn't even
kissed her yet, though he was dying to. But he couldn't
help it. He wanted people to be as kind to her as she
was to them, and expect for Winterberg, who seemed
to ignore her, they were.

By Saturday a little of the set was beginning to take
shape. Tools and lumber littered the stage; he'd heard
one old hand say they'd have it all put together in
another week. Booker had seen the set design and knew
that the one-act play took place in a gazebo and the
surrounding yard. It appeared the set was going to look
like something out of a fairy-tale book, and he wasn't
sure how he felt about standing around in the rose-
bushes and petunia plants for two hours every night
for six nights.

Not that he had a choice; he was Ken, the dull-witted
gardener, and that was that. The reason he was Ken
was so that he could remain close to Kristy. This was
something a lovesick teenager did, not a mature, hard-
bitten newspaperman. He realized his self-image was
in serious jeopardy. He also realized—due to the fact
that he'd read the entire play—that he was going to

have to stand by while Kristy tried to seduce Todd Andrews. In his script, it said he was to look jealous. Looking jealous wasn't going to be a problem.

The play was a piece a fluff, he thought. Any opportunity to say something about the human condition had been lost toward the end when Lydia puts her chin up and perseveres. Oh, well.

After Saturday's rehearsal he caught up with Kristy as she walked out of the theater.

"Heading my way?" he asked.

She turned a frowning face up to his. "Huh?"

"You were a million miles away."

"I guess I was."

"I asked if you were going my way."

"What way are you going?"

"I'm not sure. What way are you going?"

Kristy laughed. Booker loved the sound. It was like music. She said, "I'm going down to the harbor to talk to that man I told you about. Tom Jones, the fisherman."

"Mind if I come along?"

"No," Kristy said.

She got into his truck, straightening out her cotton skirt with shaky hands. Booker waited until they were headed toward the harbor before he asked her why her hands were trembling and why she seemed so preoccupied.

"What am I going to say to the poor man?" she blurted out. "Excuse me, Tom, I know you're married and have a couple of kids, but could you please tell me if you were having an affair with Nancy Collins, and if so, did you break up with her, and did that subsequently drive her into such a state that she killed herself?''

''I see what you mean,'' Booker said. He thought for a moment and added, ''Maybe this is a job for a man to handle.''

Out of the corners of his eyes, he saw Kristy look at him. ''Oh?''

''Would you be willing to let me try?''

Kristy thought of the way he'd handled Ida Collins. She said, ''What do you want me to do?''

''Hold my hands as we walk down the dock, stand around batting your eyelashes at me while we visit with him for a second, then when I pinch you, walk away for a while.''

''Sounds interesting. Are you sure all the eyelash-batting and hand-holding are really necessary?''

''Don't you want to be able to put poor Ida Collins's mind at ease?'' he asked, but ruined the serious question with a sudden grin. ''Besides, it'll be fun.''

''Hm—By the way, how does Ida's furniture look in your house?''

''There are only about ten pieces I can use, but one of those is a bed, so at least I'm off the floor. I don't know what possessed me to buy such a huge place.''

''You told me you bought it because of all the wonderful trees,'' Kristy reminded him.

Booker nodded as he pulled the truck to a stop beside three other trucks, all infected with rust. He opened Kristy's door, and as they walked down the dock, he felt her take his hand and squeeze it. He looked down into her incredibly blue eyes and smiled, hoping that at least some of the reason she bumped her hip against his had to do with him and not their search for the right Tom.

"That's his boat, the *Advance*," Kristy whispered. Seeing as her face was tilted up to his, and just in case anyone was watching, Booker leaned down and kissed her lips. He could feel her intake of breath, see the surprise flower in her eyes. He fancied he saw something else in her eyes as well, but they were at the *Advance's* side, and it was time to go to work. Discovering if he was right about the something else would have to wait.

"Look, honey, a fishing boat," Kristy said. She yanked on his hand until they were by the wide afterdeck. Booker saw a middle-aged man with thick fingers working on a line. He was a good-looking man in a ruddy, outdoorsy way. He was half sitting on a raised hatch, one foot propped on an overturned fish box. A knit fisherman's hat was pulled over his head, but a rim of blondish hair could be seen around his neck.

"Catch any fish?" Kristy called.

The man looked at them. Booker could actually see him deciding they were hopeless land-loving nonfishermen in a blink of an eye. He said, "Now there, miss, salmon season isn't open yet."

Kristy laughed. It wasn't her genuine laugh. Booker was somewhat distracted by the fact that he realized this. She elbowed him as if to remind him he was supposed to be helping in this charade.

"Bet it's great reeling in those big chinooks all summer long," he said and then kissed the top of Kristy's head. Her arm was around his waist—another distraction—and his was around her shoulders.

"Well, just like anything else, it gets to be work," Tom Jones said. "What with all the government regulations we got now, it's a wonder we get out to fish at all."

Booker nodded. "Isn't that the truth. Everytime you turn around, there's another regulation to worry about. Seems to me we have too many rules and laws in this country."

The fisherman was paying more attention to Booker now. He said, "You wouldn't believe some of the crazy things we have to do."

"Is that right?" Booker pinched Kristy gently, giving her her cue to scoot. "Tell me about them," he said.

"I'm going to go look at that other boat while you men talk," Kristy said, and darned if she didn't bat her eyelashes.

Kristy wandered down to gaze at another smelly fish boat. She couldn't even hear Booker and Tom Jones talking, and it was beginning to get cold. After waiting around for fifteen minutes, she went back to the truck and got in. When she looked out at the boats, she could see the *Advance* but no one on the dock.

Another ten minutes passed. Kristy got out her script and practiced her lines. She liked all of *Someday Soon* except the ending, which she felt was a cop-out. It wasn't like James to write a "And everyone lives happily ever after" ending, and she was vaguely disappointed he had this time. Still, she knew when she auditioned what the ending was like, though she'd had no idea it would be she, as Lydia, who would have to utter the closing words.

Eventually Booker made his way back up the dock. He slid in behind the wheel, but one deep breath told Kristy he wasn't going to be driving.

He dropped the keys in her hand before she could say a word. "You drive stick shift?" he asked, his voice a little slurred.

"Sure. Let's change places."

Booker slid across the seat before Kristy could get out, pinning her against the door. "I liked kissing you," he said, his lips an inch from hers.

"What in the world happened to you in forty-five minutes?"

"Nothing," he said and hiccupped.

"My eye."

"You have the prettiest blue eyes. They remind me of those flowers. What are those flowers called, Kristy love?"

"I don't know," she said, smiling indulgently.

"Forget-me-don't," he said.

"Forget-me-not?"

"How could I forget you?" he asked and hiccupped. He ran a cool hand down her face.

She caught his hand. "Come on, Booker, sit up now so I can get out of the truck."

He dutifully sat up. Kristy got out of the truck. By the time she got back in behind the steering wheel, he'd fastened his seat belt. He hiccupped again.

Kristy started the truck and drove up the hill out of the harbor area. "So what happened?" she asked.

"My head hurts."

"What happened to make your head hurt?" she asked, knowing the answer was on his breath.

"Four shots of straight whiskey," he groaned.

"What did he say about Nancy?"

Booker sighed. "What you have down there is a real salt-of-the-earth type of guy," he said. "Salt of the earth. You wouldn't believe how hard fishing has gotten for the little guy. What's our government thinking of, letting the Russians and the Japanese—"

"Booker, I mean what did Tom say about Nancy?"

"Oh. He said you were very pretty. That was after he invited me aboard for something to warm me up. I agreed, of course. That you were pretty, I mean. One thing led to another. We had a couple of drinks. I let him think I was married but not to you. He told me I'd be punished me for my sins. In fact, he went on and on about it. Told me he'd been led astray ten years ago, but it had only happened once and he'd begged forgiveness. He said he'd sooner be run over by a truck than fall into that trap again, and if I knew what was good for me, I'd come to church with him tomorrow."

"Good heavens, Booker. This is a tiny little town. What is he going to think when one of his kids comes through one of my classes?"

"His kids are all grown-up. Shirley is a dental hygienist, and Ben runs an ice-cream store down in Fresno. His wife, her name is Betty, has a part-time job at a fabric store. She never used to have to work, but with what's happening in the fishing industry, they need her paycheck to make the boat payments."

Kristy, open-mouthed, stared at Booker. "Good grief," she said. "You guys really did talk."

"Yeah. Tom's a real salt-of-the-earth kind of guy."

"I think you said that."

Booker groaned. "I'm not used to straight shots of liquor, you know, especially not four of them, pow, pow, pow. Wait, that's one short. Pow."

Laughing, Kristy said, "Did you have to keep up with him?"

"Hey! He was pouring, and if I didn't drink, he stared at me until I did. Since I was pumping him, it seemed like a good idea to go along. I was only trying to be polite."

"You're right," Kristy admitted, smiling to herself as he hiccupped for about the fiftieth time. "I'll question the other Tom," she added. "He's only a kid, and I'll have to go to the software store he works at, but you've already gone beyond the call of duty."

She was answered with a gentle snore and turned to see Booker slumped against his window, fast asleep.

Software Galore was a computer-software store located in the mini-mall near the one-and-only large chain grocery store in Cypress Hill. Kristy walked there from her house. The day was cold and blustery, and she quickly caught her windblown hair in a ponytail before going through the door.

There was only one other customer in the store, a girl of about twelve. Tom Savage was helping her pick out a game. Kristy stared at a display of computer diskettes until the girl made her selection and Tom rang up the sale.

"Now, ma'am, may I help you?" he asked Kristy.

His eyes widened when she turned to face him and he recognized his old teacher.

"Miss Wilder! Hey, I didn't know you have a computer."

"My kid brother has one," Kristy said. "Can you recommend a game for him? He's about fifteen."

"Oh, sure. Come over here."

Tom Savage was about six foot three, a tall beanpole of a boy with a prominent Adam's apple and a ready smile. While Kristy looked at the colorful boxes, she said, "Did you know Nancy Collins?"

"The lady that fell off of that balcony?" Tom asked.

"Yes, that's the one."

"No, I sure didn't. She was pretty old, wasn't she?"

"About my age," Kristy said, smothering a smile. "I just thought I heard someone mention you and she were friends."

"Nancy Collins? No. Maybe my mother knew her, though. She knows lots of the older ladies. I didn't mean that you're old, Miss Wilder or that . . . Heck, you want me to ask Mom if she knew her?"

"No, that's okay," Kristy said. "It doesn't matter."

"Only thing I know is what I read in the paper. Too bad she fell. Was she a friend of yours?"

The question threw Kristy for a moment. She cleared her throat and said, "Yes, I guess she was." She was beginning to realize the word "friend" was a broad word, encompassing people as diverse as Booker and Regina and even Nancy.

Kristy paid for the game and left the store, reasonably certain Tom Savage had never been in love with Nancy Collins. The whole thing was a dead end.

Chapter Six

By the third week of rehearsals, Kristy was beginning to feel comfortable with her part. The set was completed except for a minor addition of a gardening shed off to stage left. Booker was to spend most of the play in or around the shed, and Kristy thought it was probably a good idea he'd been given little jobs to do while everyone else uttered their lines. Though he was competent as Ken, the bumbling gardener, Kristy thought he was ill at ease on the stage. He did deliver his one and only line with gusto, however.

By now most of the actors had memorized their lines, and Kristy knew as soon as the set designer and his crew had the power tools out of the way, blocking would commence.

"I need Kristy Wilder," the costume designer, Hank Roscoe, called from the audience.

Kristy was in the middle of a scene with Summer. James said, "Go on, Kristy. I think it's entirely possible we can get along without you for a while."

Kristy nodded. She was determined James's biting tongue wouldn't reduce her to tears, but it was difficult at best. Summer smiled warmly at her, and Kristy followed Hank through the theater and lobby and up the stairs to the costume room which was located behind the light-and-sound booth. Hank produced a key and opened the door to the large, dry room which was visually reduced in size by the racks, stacks, boxes, and shelves of the clothes, hats, belts, shoes, purses, and odds and ends the theater owned and stored.

"Lydia, Lydia," Hank mumbled to himself as he picked a long dress off the work table beside the ironing board and sewing machine. He'd taken Kristy's measurements the first week of rehearsals. "Put this on," Hank said, handing Kristy the dress. She went behind the tacked-up sheet which created the informal dressing room, took off her own clothes, and pulled on the dress.

It was a gossamer creation of white and pale pink netting with a high neckline and full, fluttering sleeves. Kristy held up the long skirt and parted the curtain.

"Come on out here and stand on this little stool," Hank said impatiently. "Geez, I got that an acre too long, didn't I?"

"It *is* a little long," Kristy said as she stepped onto the stool.

"Guess I was thinking of Summer," Hank said idly, then seemed to realize what he'd said and glanced swiftly into Kristy's eyes. "Sorry," he mumbled.

"Listen," Kristy snapped, "I'm as surprised I was cast as Lydia as everyone else is. I don't know why James chose me, but unless I quit, there's not a thing I can do about it, and I'm no quitter."

Hank nodded slowly. "I really am sorry I made that crack about the dress," he said slowly. "I worked with you on *Tree Tops*, Kristy, so I should have figured out by now that you're not the kind to stab someone in the back. Not like some people.''

Kristy blinked away two teardrops. ''I'm the one who's sorry,'' she said. ''I shouldn't have barked at you like that. But what do you mean, 'not the kind to stab someone in the back like some people'?''

''Oh, you know,'' he said, getting down on his knees to pin the hem.

''No, I don't.''

Hank looked up at her downturned face. ''I wouldn't want to speak ill of the dead,'' he said evasively.

''Nancy? You think Nancy would have stabbed someone in the back to get what she wanted?''

Laughing softly, Hank said, ''Don't you?''

''I don't know,'' Kristy said.

''Turn around a little—that's enough,'' he directed. ''Well, trust me, she'd do whatever she had to do to get a part. I heard rumors about what she did to get the role of the sister in *Tree Tops*.''

''This place is a veritable gold mine of rumors,'' Kristy pointed out, ''especially about Nancy Collins. I've heard she drank, that she ran around, that she was suicidal—''

''So some of the rumors were obviously true,'' Hank said.

''Yes.''

''But some of them weren't.''

Kristy turned again. ''What do you mean by that?''

''Nothing.''

''Hank, do you have any idea who the Tom she was so in love with actually was? I'd like to ask him a few questions, see if I can figure out what made Nancy take that jump. Not for myself, you understand, but Nancy's mother is so upset, she put her house up for sale and left town. I'd like to help her.''

Hank opened his mouth, but before he said anything, he looked over his shoulder toward the stairs. It was a dramatic gesture that made a shiver of suspense race up Kristy's spine. He shook his head. ''Not now,'' he whispered. Kristy understood why he stalled a moment later when Rona Barnett, who was playing the part of Gloria, the maid, entered the room. Kristy hadn't heard her coming, but Hank's ears were well attuned to the small theater, and she guessed he was aware of almost everything that happened here.

''Don't you need to fit me now?'' Rona asked. ''I hope this time the dress fits. Honestly! There I was, the star of *Tree Tops*, wearing a dress that was too tight!'' Her voice faded as she bent to inspect a long row of shoes.

''If she hadn't eaten like a horse after the final fitting, it wouldn't have been too tight,'' Hank muttered as he put the last pins in Kristy's hem. ''You can take it off now,'' he said, his voice back to normal volume. ''It looks great on you—doesn't it, Rona?''

Rona spared Kristy a quick look. ''It'll do. What about mine, Hank? Hurry, I must not keep our director waiting.''

''Just a moment,'' Hank said. ''Kristy, before you change, try on this fur coat. Lydia is supposed to be dripping with money. I hope this fits; it's the smallest one we have.''

Kristy put the heavy black fur on over the dress. The hem almost brushed the floor.

"I knew it," Hank said. "Maybe I could pin it up—"

"Wait a second," Kristy said. "I have a fur coat at home that fits me to a T. I'll bring it in tomorrow night, and you can see what you think." Behind them, Rona gasped, apparently amazed Kristy should have anything as grand as a fur coat. Kristy lowered her voice so that only Hank could hear her and added, "It's a fake."

Looking toward Rona's back, Hank put his finger to his lips; then he raised his voice and said, "That'll be marvelous!"

"I also have a five-carat diamond ring," Kristy said. "Do you think Lydia would enjoy waving that around?"

Hank beamed. "Absolutely. But, Kristy, make sure it's insured before you bring it here."

"Of course," Kristy said, enjoying the conspiratorial wink Hank added for her eyes only. Rona was silent; tomorrow Kristy decided she'd share her joke, but for tonight it was kind of fun putting one over Rona, and Hank was obviously getting a real charge out of it.

"And I'll have your hat ready tomorrow night. What do you think?"

Kristy looked at the round, black spongy serving platter of a hat that was almost completely covered with vivid pink silk flowers. "It's noticeable," she said with a chuckle. "The roses almost look real."

"Illusion, my dear, illusion," Hank said. "Theater is all illusion." And with this, he gave Kristy another sly wink.

As Kristy put her own clothes back on, she felt that

little tingle of worry reenter her mind. What did Hank know or suspect? Did he possibly have the clue that would be the key to explaining why Nancy—vain, self-assured Nancy—killed herself over a man no one knew? She was determined to talk to him again and hung around for a while, but Rona wasn't satisfied with her costume. Kristy left. It would have to wait.

She ran into Regina Winterberg right outside the costume-room door. For a second they stood staring at each other. Kristy wondered if she looked as cornered as Regina did.

"I was . . . coming to get you," Regina said at last. "James wants you on stage."

Kristy nodded. "Regina, please, don't leave yet. I . . . I've been wanting to talk to you."

Regina's eyebrows arched. "Oh?"

Aware of how sounds carried, Kristy moved toward the light-and-sound room. "I don't know what's happened between James and me, why he gave me the part of Lydia, why he's so angry—"

"You're imagining things," Regina interrupted.

Kristy swallowed. "I don't think I am. But I can handle his anger. I just want to know if he told you I called one night to speak to you. The night before auditions."

"Yes," Regina said softly. "He told me you called."

"I wasn't going to tell him a thing about your baby," Kristy said softly. "I was worried about your health, that's all. I was going to ask him to encourage you to see a doctor for fatigue. But the next day you looked so much better—"

"That you decided you didn't need to speak to him,'' she interrupted again. "Kristy, Kristy. You really are imagining things. James is tense about the play—you know how he gets. You make a beautiful Lydia. Trust his judgment and stop worrying about it. And, dear Kristy, I know you wouldn't have spilled the beans about the baby."

Kristy sighed and smiled at the same time. "It's such a relief to hear you say that."

"You should have talked to me before this. Now, you'd better get on down to the stage before he really does go on the warpath."

The two women hooked arms and descended the stairs together. Kristy felt as though a huge weight had been lifted from her heart.

After rehearsal Kristy waited in the lobby for Hank. When he didn't come, she ran up the stairs to look for him, but the door to the costume room was locked. Kristy went back downstairs and into the theater. James and Regina were on the stage, talking to Rona and Duncan Barnett.

Kristy waited for a few minutes for them to finish speaking to one another. Eventually the two couples separated, and she said, "Excuse me. Has anyone seen Hank?"

"Not since the costume room," Rona said.

"Why do you want him?" James asked.

"Just to talk," Kristy said, surprised James had asked her a question. It was the first time he'd spoken to her about anything other than the play in days.

Maybe Regina had spoken to him; if so, Kristy owed her a word of thanks.

"You two were chatting up a storm," Rona said. She turned to her husband and added, "They were discussing all the rumors about you know who."

"Rona, please," Kristy said.

"Oh, I'm not going to blab. To tell you the truth, I didn't even hear what Hank was saying about Nancy, just that this rumor was true and that one wasn't. Anyway, I haven't seen him since then."

"I think he left," Duncan said.

Kristy wanted to say, "Then why in the world didn't you tell me that right away?" She said, "Thanks, Duncan," and walked away, strangely uncomfortable.

It was Monday night, so Booker hadn't been at rehearsal. Since his part was so much smaller than hers, he didn't attend every evening like she did. No doubt he was buried in his newspaper office, working on the next edition of the *Tribune*. Kristy had to admit to a chuckle or two over his predicament with the Ask Addie column. Each week the letters seemed more strange and the answers more satirical. For instance, the week before he'd told a woman who was upset with her husband because he refused to bathe to "Push him in a lake, a river, or better yet, the ocean. If he can't swim, your problems will be over."

A. W. Booker. What did the A. W. stand for, and why wouldn't he tell her? She smiled warmly and lay back on her bed. They still hadn't kissed, unless you counted the little peck down at the harbor. She'd purposely avoided being in situations with him where they'd be alone, but if asked why, she'd be hard pressed for an answer.

He was beautiful, she thought, with his strong body, wide shoulders, deep-brown eyes. She liked the way the hair grew on his arms, the way his chin and jaw jutted forward a little, the angles of his cheekbones. She liked the feel of his hands and his lips, the interest on his face when she spoke to him. She'd asked him if he'd ever been married, and he'd said once, unsuccessfully. She'd liked the way he didn't try to blame the breakup on Catherine, his ex-wife, and the way he added, "We were just too young to realize how different we were."

There wasn't much she didn't like about him. And that, in a nutshell, was why she was purposely keeping him at arm's length. He was a man in every sense of the word, from the strength of his character and convictions to the way he spoke frankly and honestly with the people around him, to the way he made her feel when he looked at her. He was exactly the kind of man she wanted for the long run, but she wasn't at all sure he was interested in such a thing. In fact, she suspected he was more of a sprinter. It would be easy to get lost in those brown eyes, easy to surrender to those strong arms, but what would she do when it was over for him?

Not yet, she told herself.

Meanwhile, it wasn't as though there weren't a million other things to do. There were finals to prepare for at school, the matter of Nancy's suicidal plunge to unravel for Ida, the play which opened in two weeks, her neglected home which was cluttered with all the things she'd been too preoccupied the last few weeks to put away. Of all those things, it was the clutter that was the easiest to deal with, so she got to her feet and began sorting the papers on her desk.

An hour later she found the oak slab which constituted the top of the desk. She dusted it, took a deep breath of satisfaction, and tackled the kitchen table. That took longer as she ran across a stack of poems written by her second-period creative-writing class. She'd forgotten about the poems, so she sat down and, in a fit of guilt, read them all, hastily scrawling notes in the margins, each comment as positive as she could make it.

After the table, she moved onto her bedroom where she changed the sheets, then tackled the stack of clothes thrown onto the rocker during the past several days. Under the clothes she found the briefcase Ida Collins had insisted Kristy take home and use. She'd dumped it on the chair that night and covered it with clothes the next.

Nancy's briefcase. Kristy picked it up and sat down on the chair, the briefcase in her lap. She ran her hands over the smooth burgundy leather. It was a suitcase-type briefcase, the kind with two gold snaps and tumble locks. Kristy tried the snaps. The case was locked. Since Ida had opened it to look inside, Kristy figured she must know the combination. She made a mental note to call Booker and ask if he happened to have Ida's sister's address so she could write for the combination. For now, she stored the case in her closet.

There was no doubt at all, she reflected as she took off her work clothes and sank into a hot tub of bubbles, that talking to Regina had made her feel a million percent better. Kristy closed her eyes and leaned her head back against the tub. She'd tried calling Hank Roscoe at home, but he hadn't answered his phone. Maybe after rehearsal tomorrow she could invite him out for a drink. If he understood how haunted Ida was, he'd think of something that could help explain Nancy's decision to end her life. Or had it truly been a tragic piece of overacting—that had been Kristy's first reaction to it. For now, it was still the only thing that made any sense.

Thinking of Nancy made Kristy think about Charlie Hook and Jim Turner. She hoped they were getting on with their lives. This train of thought was interrupted by the doorbell.

Kristy sat up. She picked her watch off of the counter and saw that it was after ten o'clock, kind of late for unannounced callers. Occasionally, however, a desperate student begged their case at an ungodly hour, and seeing as a big paper on American poets was due tomorrow, she wouldn't be surprised if this was the case.

Wrapped in a white cotton robe, her damp hair pinned atop her head, Kristy answered the door.

Booker grinned. "Ah, a gift-wrapped beauty just for me."

Kristy felt her heartbeat accelerate. Crazy, but that was the way he made her feel: breathless, disorientated, excited.

"I was in the tub," she said. "It's kind of late."

He leaned against the doorjamb. "What if I told you

I was driving past and happened to see your light was still on?''

''I'd point out that you live in the opposite direction from the newspaper office.''

''Oh. Well, what if I said I was working late and I got to thinking about you and that got me so steamed up that I thought I'd come over here and ravage you?''

''Closer to the truth, I suppose,'' Kristy said, smiling.

''Right on the money. You're not going to invite me inside, though, are you?''

Kristy pulled the two sides of her robe closer together. ''No,'' she said.

''Why not? You're all grown up, and so am I. We're obviously attracted to each other.''

Kristy said, ''That's why.''

''What's why?''

''Everything you said. That's why I'm not inviting you inside. You scare the devil out of me.''

Booker's lips spread into a wide smile. ''I don't believe I've scared the devil out of a woman for years.'' He reached across the threshold and touched her cheek. ''You look absolutely bewitching. If I can't come inside, how about one lousy kiss?''

''I don't want a *lousy* kiss,'' Kristy said softly.

Booker straightened up and came a step closer. He put his hands on either side of her damp face and leaned down until his mouth closed over her mouth. Kristy felt her resolve foundering, and when one of his hands slipped down and circled her waist, pulling her so close she could feel the buttons on his jacket through her robe, she surrendered willingly. She wrapped her arms around his neck, passion making the pounding of her heart merge with his.

It was Booker who pulled away. He kissed her cheek and her eyelids, ran his hands through her hair, which had come unpinned in the embrace.

"This is not the way to get me to go home," he said huskily, his breath warm on her ear.

Kristy took a deep breath. "It's your fault. I've never been kissed like that before."

"And in an open doorway for the whole world to see," Booker said, "no doubt violating several Cypress Hill civil codes." He sighed deeply and added, "I want more of the same. I want more, period."

It took Kristy a moment to respond. "Let's get through the play first. Let's be certain about how we feel."

For several seconds she wasn't sure he was going to accept her ground rules. She wasn't even sure she wanted him to. At last he nodded. "Then I'd really better go home."

It wasn't until he was halfway down the walk that Kristy remembered the combination. "Do you have Ida's sister's address?" she called.

He turned slowly. "She wrote it on the back of my business card in case I had trouble getting the sofa to fold down into a bed." He opened his wallet and withdrew a card. When he handed it to Kristy, their fingers touched.

"I'd better go," he said, looking at their hands.

"Yes," Kristy agreed. She closed the door and leaned back against it. She was in love with him. She knew if he didn't feel the same way about her, it was going to break her heart.

The next day was one of those days every teacher has and every teacher dreads. Nothing went right. Half of her second-period class were late with their papers on American poets, Rob Stevenson and a band of his young cronies disrupted the creative-writing class to the point where Kristy gave up and assigned busy work, and the principal called two of her fourth-period seniors into his office for disciplinary actions after they went ahead and printed what he considered obscene material in the *Senior Bulletin*, an in-school newspaper Kristy had nothing to do with. Nevertheless, the rest of her fourth period went on strike to protest repression and censorship.

To top it off, there were two mandatory meetings after school, which meant she wouldn't have time for dinner before rehearsal. She munched on crackers and cheese during the second meeting, and just when she thought she was finally free of Manzanita High School for the day, another problem arose.

This time it was the parents of one of her freshman students. Mr. and Mrs. Jolliet objected to the reading material in Kristy's English class. When she tried to put them off until the next afternoon, they threatened to go to the school board.

The book they were so upset about was a collection of Chekhov plays. Kristy was eventually able to make them understand she wasn't encouraging their daughter to charge off and join the red brigade, but it took time as she had to open her classroom, produce the book, explain about Russian literature, cajole and promise and smile. By the time she finally ushered them off the school campus, she was running a half an hour behind. By the time she made it to the repertory theater, she was a full forty-five minutes late.

As Kristy walked down the aisle to the stage, she felt her spirits soar. The set really was beautiful—Len had outdone himself. Downstage right was the gazebo, a lattice-roofed structure about eight feet high, supported by four small pillars. It was left wide open so the audience's view wasn't obstructed. Behind it and running to upstage left was a rock fence covered with climbing roses, backed with trees. Stage left held the small shed Booker would lurk around and inside, and downstage center sat a small white bench.

The rest of the stage was covered with plants and grass; it truly did look like the setting for a summer garden party. And from the audience it looked like every plant had sprung from the stage, every building had been newly painted for the coming season. No one would ever suspect the rock wall was sponge-painted plywood, the climbing roses were fake, or that Mother Nature had never laid eyes on the trees.

James spared her a quick glance as Kristy approached the stage. She'd thrown the fake fur over her skirt and sweater so she wouldn't have to lug it in her arms. She was also wearing the fake diamond and looked around hastily for Hank Roscoe.

"You're late," James barked.

"I'm sorry. It was unavoidable." She sought out Booker, who winked at her. She grinned, amazed how lighthearted a wink could make a person feel.

"Just get up here," James snapped. "You've kept everyone waiting."

The lighthearted feeling fled. Kristy climbed the short flight of stairs. She felt all eyes on her as she stepped onto the stage and wasn't sure if it was because her cheeks were aflame with embarrassment over the way James spoke to her or because she looked to be wearing several thousands of dollars of mink on her back. It was impossible to blurt out her newly acquired riches were actually imitations, so she sighed heavily and crossed to center stage to stand before James.

His eyes were glued to Kristy's right hand, to the mammoth glittering cubic zirconia which caught the bright lighting and reflected it in a blaze of brilliance. The stone looked real enough to quicken the pulse of the best jeweler. Kristy smiled when his gaze reached her face.

"You're incredible," he said. "I never would have thought it of you."

Kristy didn't know what to make of his words. She said, "Hank and I thought my own . . . things . . . you know, things that fit . . . well, we thought I could wear them until I leave the stage to take off my hat. Then I could leave the coat in the dressing room."

James narrowed his eyes. "I see," he said curtly. "It seems as though a lot of your dreams are coming true lately, doesn't it?"

Kristy decided she'd liked it better when James wasn't speaking to her. For what seemed like ten minutes but was probably only ten seconds, no one spoke. Then James appeared to recapture some of his old aplomb. It was almost as though a decision had been reached, a solution decided upon.

"Okay, Act I, Scene I," he said. "Our trusty gardener Ken is stage left, potting pansies. Gloria is center stage, in the gazebo, setting out tea. Lydia enters from up right. Remember, everyone, be careful to step over the toolbox that's still there. Len assures me the workmen will get it out of here by tomorrow."

Slowly the whole cast walked through the motions as James directed them. Kristy wished she could get rid of the heavy synthetic fur, but didn't want to do anything to bring attention to herself. As she penciled her blocking directions into her script book, she caught sight of Booker staring at her hand, his eyes wide, and she giggled to herself. The stone in the ring really did look real.

"Lydia leaves up center, through the gate in the rock wall," James said. Kristy looked at the gate. A doorway had been painted beyond it; it looked for all intents and purposes like the back door to a country estate.

"She hears Ken shout, 'Look out, Miss Gloria,' " Winterberg continued. "She rushes back onstage in time to catch the maid, who has just fainted. She shouts for her secretary to come. She's annoyed she's had to pinch-hit this way—after all, a lady doesn't go around catching faint maids. Anna Thorton comes onstage for the first time. She takes Gloria backstage. The two of them come back a few minutes later when Fenton shows up and Lydia calls for them to help her set out the tea. Rona, one word of caution. Just faint. Don't do a death scene, okay? Just faint quietly and let Booker shout for help."

"I would never overact!" Rona said, apparently offended.

Kristy thought it a sign of how good the actors were getting that not a soul so much as smiled.

"Of course you wouldn't," Winterberg said appeasingly. "Okay, let's run through it. Kristy, remember to move upstage left when you call for Gloria and Anna Thorton to come back on stage the second time."

Kristy dutifully exited through the swinging gate and then through the door which led directly into a short narrow hallway that brought her directly into the dressing room backstage. She looked around for Hank, but there was no sign of him. She hung up her coat. In the future, during dress rehearsals and performances, she'd also unpin the rose-covered hat that went with the coat.

She was grateful there were no costume changes. During *Tree Tops*, all the women had had to change at least once, which meant bedlam in the dressing room. Except for Summer, Kristy recalled. Intensely modest, Summer always used the upstairs dressing room to change. Kristy looked up through the dark cracks and laughed to herself. In reality, it was better to use this hallway of a dressing room than the stuffy nether regions of the upstairs.

Kristy heard Booker say, "Look out, Gloria," and hurried to reenter the stage through the same door from which she'd left it, right on cue.

After the rehearsal was over, Hank finally appeared. "I have the hat," he said and presented the flowering masterpiece to Kristy. She put it atop her head and took the gentle ribbing of the other actors.

"It's a good thing this comes off right away," she said.

"I rather like it," Booker said, a smile lurking in the sable-brown depths of his eyes.

"It's hideous," Hank said. "Now, Kristy, did you bring your fur coat?"

"It's backstage," Kristy said and ran to get it. When she reemerged, she was wearing the hat and the coat, waving her "diamond-studded" hand out in front of her. "Darlings, don't make a fuss," she said, reciting a line directly out of the play.

"Perfect," Hank said. He looked sideways at Rona Barnett and added, "You must have come into a lot of money, Kristy. Well, never mind, if you have it, why not invest it in things that make you look as glorious as these do?"

"Indeed," Kristy said. She'd seen Hank's wink and understood he still wanted her to pretend the items were real.

Rona Barnett glared at her from across the stage. "Mink," she said as though the mere thought of such a thing was offensive. "I wouldn't be caught dead in anything but ermine. Was this hand-me-down from an aged aunt, Kristy? It does smell like mothballs, doesn't it?"

Kristy said, "Does it?"

Hank laughed, Booker raised his eyebrows, and James looked pale. Kristy was tired of the game, but she wasn't about to admit anything in front of Rona Barnett. She kept her mouth closed as the group began breaking up.

Kristy put her hand on Hank's arm. "Would you

like to go out for a drink?'' she asked. ''My treat?''
Out of the corner of her eyes she saw Booker blink
rapidly. She yearned to be with him—him and him
alone, for that matter—but this was something she felt
she had to take care of.

''Can't tonight,'' Hank said. ''I have an . . . engagement.'' He winked at her. ''Come in early tomorrow night, and we'll chat.'' He said this softly, but
the rest of the company were so quiet, Kristy felt sure
his words were heard by one and all.

''You're on.''

They walked away from everyone, and Hank whispered, ''You'd better take these things home with you.
We don't want Rona snooping.''

''Hank, I'd better warn you that the jig is almost
up. I can't keep quiet about the real nature of my 'fur
coat' and 'diamond ring.' It makes me feel as though
I'm cheating.''

Hank laughed. ''Kristy, the trouble with you is
you're too honest. Go on then. Tomorrow night you
can tell the whole assembly, but I wish you wouldn't.
It's really none of their business, and the uppity way
Rona and Duncan act toward everyone else really gets
my goat.'' He paused for a second and added, ''Besides, Winterberg thought he had you figured out, and
now he's not so sure. Serves him right, too.'' He took
back the hat. ''I've got to run,'' he said. ''See you
tomorrow night.''

Kristy left the theater through the back door. She
was almost to her car when Booker called her name.

''Now that you're wealthy, have you forgotten the
little people you knew back when?'' he asked.

"I could never forget you," Kristy said. The truth of the matter was that she'd lingered, waiting for him, until she saw that he and James were talking. Booker she'd longed to run into; James, she could do without. She'd left, disappointed.

Booker sighed. "Have you eaten? Will you let me buy you a steak at the Lonesome Tortoise?"

"Why there?" Kristy asked.

"Because it's after eleven, and I believe they're the only place in town still open. Besides, I saw in the paper that Charlie Hook is performing this week, and I wondered if we shouldn't have a little talk with him."

"Good idea," Kristy said and put her coat and ring in her car. "Shall I follow you?"

"Just come with me in the truck. We'll come back for your car afterward."

Chapter Seven

The Lonesome Tortoise was amazingly busy considering the time of night it was. Kristy didn't recognize a single soul; apparently the world she occupied as high-school teacher and community-theater actress wasn't the only world Cypress Hill had to offer. Who knew how many other Toms or Thomases there were in town and, for that matter, in the three small towns within ten miles? There were probably dozens, and her determination to find the right one seemed naive and almost impossible.

They sat at a different table, and when they went to order the same meal they'd eaten before, the waitress informed them the kitchen closed at ten o'clock. Booker pleaded their case, and pretty soon they were eating cold turkey sandwiches. The surprise was how good the sandwiches were—the turkey was real turkey, not the flattened, chopped, pressed variety Kristy so detested.

At eleven o'clock Charlie Hook took the stage. For forty minutes Kristy and Booker listened to country-influenced ballads. Charlie had a fully developed twang

120

and a way of singing that made Kristy think of a crickety front porch swing and a lazy hound dog.

When Charlie was finished singing, Booker intercepted his path to the bar. Charlie came to the table, nodded once at Kristy, and sat down. He was wearing another western shirt, this one gray with pink buttons and fringe. He took off his hat and set it on the bench next to him. His complexion was fair, his eyes a faded blue. Comparing the two men, Kristy didn't think it possible they could be less alike except that somehow they weren't. This contradiction puzzled her until she realized it was the inherent masculinity both men projected which was so similar.

"Don't I know you two from somewhere?" Charlie asked.

"We were at the Winterberg house the night Nancy died," Kristy said. "We were at the front door when you came to pick her up."

He nodded, a tight knot forming in his jaw. "That's right, I remember now. Well, what can I do for you?"

The waitress put a beer mug on the table in front of Charlie. Booker paid for it, and the waitress disappeared.

"We're trying to help Nancy's mother understand Nancy's death," Booker said. "She's having a real hard time of it."

"*She's* having a hard time," Charlie said, shaking his head. "It's about split me apart. Say, you two know anything about Nancy and some guy named Tom?"

Kristy sighed. "We were hoping you could tell us about him."

"There is no *him*," Charlie said. "There can't be. Nancy was going to marry me." He downed half the mug of beer and wiped his mouth with the back of his hand.

"I didn't know that," Kristy said. "She never mentioned your name."

"That's 'cause her mother didn't approve of me. Said what kind of a future does a singing cowboy have in Northern California? I told Nancy to tell the old bat I wasn't going to be in California for long. I had plans. I was going to marry Nancy and take her to Nashville. With her looks and my voice, I was sure we could get an act together or something." He sighed heavily and added, "I sure miss that little gal."

"Had you asked her to marry you?"

"Not yet, but she knew I was going to. She teased me about it."

"And she never mentioned anyone named Tom?" Booker asked.

"Heck, no! Between her job and acting in that play which took just about all her time, when did she have time to run around with someone else? She didn't. The only other man I ever saw hang around her was that Jim Turner. She broke up with him when the two of us met, and he couldn't accept it. But he's a mild little man. Tried to punch me out the other night and ended up in a sorrowful heap of tears. Pitiful sight."

"It doesn't make sense," Kristy said through a yawn as Booker drove her back to her car.

"No, it doesn't. She was apparently keeping Charlie

Hook a secret. It seems strange she'd keep two men dangling.''

Kristy nodded, too tired to think or talk. She was intensely aware of Booker's presence so close to her. All night she'd longed to be in his arms, and the kiss they'd shared on her doorstep the night before had played itself over and over in her mind like a favorite scene from a beloved movie. Part of her was ready for the sequel, and part of her was still scared of the man she found so intriguing.

"That was quite some entrance you made at the theater tonight," Booker said. "You should have seen Winterberg's eyes. I guess everyone had you figured as a poor little schoolteacher, and in you walk looking like a million bucks."

"What did you think?" Kristy asked as they passed the front of the theater. Hank Roscoe's red minivan was parked on the street, and for an instant Kristy toyed around with the idea of banging on the theater door to see if Hank was still inside. She abandoned the idea immediately; if he was upstairs, he wouldn't hear her knocking, and besides, she was just too tired.

"Do you want the truth?" Booker asked as he pulled his truck up alongside her car and turned off the engine.

"Of course."

He was silent for several seconds, his profile turned to Kristy as he stared straight ahead. The only light in the cab came from a street lamp, and as it was half a block away, it didn't do much to illuminate his face. At last he cleared his throat and turned to face her.

"I was jealous," he said.

"Jealous!"

"You wanted the truth. I know what you do for a living, the kind of car you drive, the place you call home. They're all very nice, but nothing prepared me for a diamond the size of a golf ball and a full-length fur coat. To tell you the truth, I never figured you as the fur-coat kind."

"I'm not," Kristy said. "I detest the whole idea of fur coats."

He put his hand toward her, and she took it. He brought her hand back to his face and kissed the inside of her wrist. "I assumed someone else bought you the fur and the diamond."

"Someone else did," Kristy said truthfully.

"Kristy Wilder, are you trying to drive me crazy?"

She laughed softly. "I've heard jealousy is an indication of self-doubt," she said. "I never would have figured you for self-doubt."

He pulled on her arm until she was by his side. He put a stop to her laughing by kissing her soundly on the mouth. The kiss wasn't as tender as the one the night before, and somehow that made it all the more exciting. It was Kristy who applied the brakes.

"I'll bet this time we're violating vehicular laws or something," she said breathlessly.

"I don't care," he told her. "I just don't want other men buying you presents. I don't want other men looking at you, for that matter. Take that Roscoe character. Why are you and he arranging a little chat tomorrow night? Don't answer that," he said as she started to explain. "It's none of my business. I don't know why I'm acting like this."

Kristy peered into his eyes, wishing it weren't so blasted dark. "Don't you?" she asked at last.

A long silence followed. Kristy realized immediately how her words had sounded—exactly as she meant them. But she hadn't meant to ask for a verbal confirmation of his feelings so soon, especially when she really wasn't ready to offer one herself.

"It's getting late," he finally said, opening the door.

Kristy scooted behind the wheel and got out his door as it was closer. She unlocked her car and got inside, avoiding Booker's gaze.

"Good night," Booker said.

"See you tomorrow night," she mumbled, and started her car. A lot of his questions had been left unanswered—for instance, about the fur and the diamond and her reason for seeking a chat with Hank Roscoe. But her unasked question had been answered. Her instincts about his motives had been right. Thank goodness she'd found out now before she got more deeply involved. Booker wasn't ready for love, at least not for the kind of love Kristy would have to demand. She couldn't take less than she was willing to give and still respect herself, but as she drove away, huge tears gathered in her eyes and flowed unheeded down her cheeks.

Booker cursed himself all the way home. He cursed himself as he took a shower, and then as he lay in Ida Collins's old bed, he decided to blame Kristy for the crummy way he was feeling.

"Don't you?" she'd asked. Don't you know why you're jealous and acting like a love sick boy? Don't you know why you feel it's okay to ask me personal questions and act as though we're bound at the hip even though we've only shared three meals and as many kisses?

She hadn't said most of that, of course, but that's what had been behind her words.

Who had been giving her expensive presents? Hank Roscoe? Could it possibly be Hank Roscoe? The man was old enough to be her father and about as romantic as Captain Kangaroo.

On the other hand, Booker reminded himself, what did he know about what made a man romantic to a woman? Oh, this was insane! He'd told himself this Wilder woman was going to be nothing but trouble, and sure enough, he'd been right.

But had he been smart enough to evade her trap? Had he run when she batted those blue eyes at him, taken cover when she melted into his arms? Here he was, a full-grown man with a sour marriage and a respectable trail of beautiful women behind him, and he'd fallen prey to a little schoolteacher!

She'd acted helpless in his arms, while all the time it was he who was helpless in hers! He punched the extra pillow and hugged it to his chest. Maybe it was time to leave Kristy Wilder alone. Maybe it was time to get back to concentrating on the newspaper. He needed to find someone else to write the Ask Addie column. He wanted to devote time to covering the real stories of the area, stories like the one he could sense behind the plight of the local fishermen, a story which had suggested itself when he talked with Tom Jones. He'd wanted to run his ideas by Kristy, who was so much more in tune with this little town than he was, but he wouldn't now.

And, he remembered with a deep sigh, he needed to make it through Winterberg's stupid play with the wishy-washy ending. He didn't have time to try to figure out fickle women with big blue eyes and soft golden curls.

Kristy got through the next day at school by not thinking about anything but her students. She was honest enough to admit to herself that they'd been about third on her list of priorities lately, and she was determined to rectify it. But after school, as she began looking over the poetry papers, she thought about her coming meeting with Hank Roscoe. She left the school early, grabbed a hot bowl of soup at home, and walked to the theater, arriving a half hour before schedule.

As she walked, she thought about Booker, annoyed that the mere thought of him brought tears to her eyes. She resolutely brushed them away. Trouble was, there was no avoiding him. The play opened in less than two weeks, so from now on she'd have to see him every day. How was she going to stand a few feet away from him, talk to him, know he was watching her every movement because he had to, it was part of his character? What had possessed her to ask him if he loved her, for that's exactly how her question had come out. She'd ruined everything, for obviously he didn't and she'd forced his hand. The future suddenly looked long and lonely.

I was afraid of him, she thought, *and now I've made him afraid of me.*

Kristy knocked on the stage door. The stage manager, Jack Osborne, a big bear of a man with a bald head and a penchant for wearing overalls, opened it for her.

"A little early tonight, aren't we?" he asked as Kristy squeezed past him, her arms loaded with the big fake fur. This thing was going to get deposited upstairs—she was finished dragging it back and forth.

"I need to talk with Hank Roscoe. Do you know where he is?"

"I haven't seen him tonight, but his car was out front when I got here, so I assume he's upstairs in the costume room. By the way, I guess congratulations are in order."

This stopped Kristy. She looked over her shoulder and said, "What do you mean?"

"I mean your sudden wealth. I heard you won the lottery or inherited a bundle from an aunt."

Kristy laughed. "Rumors. I'm as broke as always."

He looked at her hand and the coat over her arm and raised a pair of bushy eyebrows.

"Oh, that," she said wearily. Until she spoke to Hank, she felt duty bound to maintain the illusion, but she shook her head. "Things aren't always as they appear," she said mysteriously.

Jack threw back his head and laughed. "What a line! Well, I bear you no ill will, Kristy."

Why did things just seem to get more and more complicated? Kristy thought. She started to walk away.

"Listen, as long as I have you here, I wanted to ask you a question," Jack said.

She felt her heart race. There were too many subjects she didn't really want to talk about. She said, "Oh?"

"Yeah. A big old pipe wrench disappeared out of one of the carpenters' toolboxes the other day. I'm asking around to see if anyone has seen it. I asked the others last night, but you were late getting here."

"I'm sorry," Kristy told him, relieved the question was an easy one to answer. "I haven't seen any stray tools."

"Well, if you do—"

"I'll let you know." She left her things in the dressing room and walked quickly through the theater and lobby. The stairs leading up to the light-and-sound booth and the costume-design room beyond were dark. Kristy flicked on the light and climbed the stairs. The door to the costume room was locked.

Kristy knocked. "Hank?" She knew it was silly to knock as the lock was hooked on the outside of the door. She left, a little annoyed and a little worried. She propped the front door of the theater open and looked out on the street. Sure enough, Hank's red minivan was parked along the curb in the same place it had been the night before. Kristy peered in the ticket office window. Greta Sanders wasn't in the office—no reason why she should be—and it was dark. Kristy went back inside the theater.

The rehearsal went well. The play was only an hour and fifteen minutes long, and the blocking was simple. Since Kristy had first seen a copy of the play, James had rewritten a few of the lines in the ending, but the fact remained that it lacked any real punch. Lydia, unloved by Fenton, coveted only by a gardener she

didn't know existed, gave a defiant little speech, held
her chin high, and—in the vein of plucky heroines
everywhere from Scarlet O'Hara to Auntie Mame—
told Anna Thorton to start a guest list for a garden
party. Life was a party!

Kristy delivered her last line, and Regina, who had
started coming to all the rehearsals, clapped. Kristy
looked around at the other actors and felt she could
read the expression on their faces: disappointment.
Shouldn't Lydia crumble a little? Couldn't her pride
slip for a moment? Wouldn't it be more interesting if
Fenton was actually in love with Anna Thorton or,
heaven forbid, even Gloria, the maid? What if Lydia
found out? What would she do?

All these ideas stayed locked in Kristy's head. James
Winterberg was finally treating her halfway decently,
and she wasn't going to butt into something that wasn't
any of her business. Besides, the board of directors
had chosen *Someday Soon* as a prize winner, and she
could only assume they knew more about plays than
she did.

"Pretty good, pretty good," James said. He glanced
at his notes, but before he could speak again, Jack
Osborne approached him.

"Found this on my desk," the burly stage manager
said as he handed Winterberg an envelope. "Don't ask
me where it came from because I don't know." He
turned to everyone else and added, "Anyone found
that pipe wrench yet?

No one had. "Thanks, anyway," he said. "And
before you leave, did anyone see Hank Roscoe tonight?"

"He didn't show up?" Kristy asked. She glanced at Booker, but his gaze was directed toward the center of the stage.

"Nope. Dress rehearsal tomorrow night, too. Not like him not to show."

"You're losing everything, Jack," Summer said. "First the wrench and now poor Hank."

Jack laughed good-naturedly and left. Kristy glanced at Booker again—it was habitual; she couldn't seem to stop doing it—and found his face set in a scowl. At least he wasn't scowling at her. She turned to see what was making him frown and saw James standing center stage, the envelope in one hand, a piece of paper in the other. His face was easily as white as the paper.

"Rehearsal is over," he said abruptly, casting Kristy a venomous look that made her knees feel like buckling. Kristy looked out into the audience. Regina, knitting needles aside, was leaning over the seat in front of her, her eyes worried as she looked at her husband.

As the other actors dispersed, Kristy took an awkward step toward James. She had no idea what was in the letter, but she couldn't bear the thought of further misunderstandings between them.

"James," she began, one hand outstretched.

He crumbled up the paper and stuck it in his pocket. Without addressing her, he stalked off the stage. Kristy looked out in the audience, but Regina was gone. She felt huge tears burning the back of her nose, sobs aching to burst from her chest, but she fought to stay in control. There was nowhere private to turn. Actors and stage-hands were backstage, the theater was wide open, technicians were upstairs. She didn't even have a car to retreat to.

And then she felt him behind her. Without turning, she knew who it was. She felt his hands on her arms as he gently turned her, and then, confronted with his wide chest and strong shoulders, she collapsed into his arms and cried.

"It's all right," Booker whispered against her hair.

Kristy felt as though a flood dam had burst. She couldn't seem to get herself under control. She felt him press a handkerchief into her hands, and she used it to mop up between quiet sobs only Booker could hear. When at last she seemed to be cried out, Booker said, "May I give you a ride home? I think we need to talk."

Kristy nodded. She retrieved her belongings and followed him out to his truck. As she looked at the theater, she wondered how she was ever going to have the nerve to walk back through the doors again. It wasn't until they drove by the front of the theater and she saw Hank's minivan that she remembered he had never appeared.

Booker drove slowly, heading toward the beach. It wasn't late—Winterberg had dismissed everyone unexpectedly early—but it was dark. Beside him sat Kristy, her hands folded in her lap, staring straight ahead.

He had had no intention of being alone with her tonight, but the expression on her face when Winterberg walked away had torn at his heart, and a few fuzzy notions in the back of his mind had crystalized.

"You were right," he said.

Kristy took a deep breath. When she spoke, her voice sounded strangely subdued. "I was right about what?" she asked.

He didn't answer her. He knew every word counted. There wasn't room for evasions anymore, and if he blew it this time, she might bolt for good. He said, "Do you mind if I park here?"

"I don't even know where we are."

Booker stopped the truck. "The sign says Bearclaw Beach. Would you like to take a walk?"

Kristy said, "Why not?"

He came around and opened her door. The wind had come up, and it was cold. "Put on your fur," he told her. "It's cold out here."

"The coat is a fake," Kristy said woodenly. "So is the ring."

"The coat will keep you warm, fake or not," Booker told her as he held it open and she slipped it over her arms. He couldn't believe how good it made him feel to know the coat and the ring were phonies.

Booker pulled a sweater over his own head, and they began walking along the road. It was too dark to get over to the beach, but the road was seldom used, and at least they could hear the waves crashing against the sand. Booker put his arm around Kristy's shoulders. He felt her shiver at his touch. They kept walking until they were in danger of running out of road.

Now was as good a time as ever. Booker took a deep breath and said, "Like I said earlier, you were perfectly right. About me, that is. About why I'm jealous."

Kristy shrugged. "I shouldn't have pressured you. I didn't mean to, really. But it all seemed so obvious to me."

"I'm in love with you," he blurted out, mentally kicking himself because it was hardly the way he'd planned to tell her. On the other hand, the plan was only about thirty minutes old and his stomach hurt. Even breathing was difficult, and he realized suddenly he was holding his breath. He let it out slowly. Had he just told Kristy Wilder he loved her?

Kristy had taken a few steps back. Her hair caught the moonlight. Her face was a delicate pale oval, her eyes deep hollows. She said, "You're what?"

This time he took a deep breath. "I'm in love with you," he repeated. "You know I am, Kristy. You said as much last night and I clammed up. I don't know exactly why I love you unless it's the way I feel when I'm around you, the way you make me feel. I think about you all the time, even when I try not to. It's occurred to me the only way I'm ever going to get my life back on track is to be near you as much as possible, to love you, to try to make you love me. I don't know why you should love me, I really don't, but, Kristy, here I am with my heart on my sleeve."

"Oh, Booker," she whispered as she came into his arms. He found her mouth and kissed her; he loved her so much it hurt, so intensely it overwhelmed him. Feeling this way was scary and intoxicating at the same time. But it was important she understand, so he forced himself to release her, to hold her hands and try to explain.

"You know about my first marriage. What you don't

know is what a failure I felt like when Catherine left. It took me years to understand it wasn't my fault, and I swore on a stack of Bibles that I would never, ever be caught in such an emotional booby-trap again. I've dated a lot of women in the last five years, Kristy, nice women, rotten apples, the whole spectrum. But I never let them get close. You're different.''

''I love you,'' she said. ''That's why I'm different.''

He laughed. ''Maybe. There's just something about you. It's in your hair and the way you walk, even the way you smell, like cool water and sunshine. I can't bear to think of the future without you. Can you possibly understand how terrifying this whole thing is to me? I mean, I thought I loved Catherine, yet that was nothing, *nothing* compared to this.''

''It's terrifying for me, too,'' Kristy said. ''I'm twenty-six years old, and I've never been in love. Part of me thought I never was going to be in love and that the wise thing to do was to find myself a good cat and devote myself to teaching. The other part of me said to wait, that someone special would show up one day, that I'd know the first time I saw him. But it didn't happen like that. I liked what I saw, of course, but you kept growing on me, Booker.''

''Like mold?''

''Like mold,'' she agreed with a smile in her voice.

And then they were in each other's arms again. Eventually they began the long walk back to the truck. She told him about Hank Roscoe. He listened to her, his hand wrapped tightly around hers. He wasn't sure exactly what was going on at the theater, but he did know this: He loved this woman, and together they'd unravel this current mystery. And if Winterberg didn't stop hurting Kristy, he, A. W. Booker, was personally going to rearrange the man's face.

He told Kristy this last thought as it was burning through his gut and he had to get it out. She laughed, a sound he'd thought he might never hear again, and told him it was all right.

"No, it's not. I don't know what's in those notes the man keeps getting, but it's obvious it's got something to do with you. I'm not going to stand by while he makes you cry, Kristy."

"What could be in the notes?" Kristy asked. "Honest, Booker, I have no guilty secrets to hide."

"He doesn't act as though it's something *about* you, anyway, does he? He looks at you as though you're responsible for the notes."

Kristy said, "You're right, but it's impossible."

"You can't think of anything?"

"Not a thing. Listen, Booker, I'm going to break my word and repeat something I promised I wouldn't. Regina Winterberg is pregnant."

"Why are they keeping it such a secret?"

"It's Regina. She told me the night Nancy died, but she made me promise not to tell her husband. Maybe this all has something to do with that and nothing to do with me. In fact, when I asked Regina what was wrong with James, she told me it was all in my imagination."

Booker frowned. He was glad Kristy couldn't see his face because if she could see his expression, he was sure she'd realize he didn't believe a word of it. He'd seen anger and hate on faces before—in his business it was sometimes a daily occurrence—and that was exactly the way Winterberg had looked at Kristy when he opened the second envelope. It had made all of Booker's protective feelings for Kristy bubble to the surface, had dashed away any residual fear of commitment, had solidified the way he felt about her. For that, he supposed he owed Winterberg a hearty thank-you; somehow he didn't feel like offering it.

He cleared his throat. "On a calmer note, what were you and Hank going to talk about tonight?"

"Nancy. He told me some of the rumors about her were true and some weren't. I was going to ask him to explain himself. You know, it's very strange about his car being at the theater. The stage manager said it was there when he arrived earlier this evening. In fact, I saw it last night when you and I drove by."

"Maybe he had car trouble and his date last night gave him a ride home. Maybe he's stuck at his home without transportation. Do you know where he lives?"

"Not far from here," Kristy said. "I went to a party at his house about two months ago."

"Want to go by his house and check on him?"

"Would you mind?"

"Not at all, especially if it will ease your mind." He waited a second and added, "So the diamond and fur are phonies, huh?"

"My mother is addicted to television shopping. Are you disappointed?"

"What do you think?"

"I think I'm going to love you forever," she said.

Booker stopped walking. He pulled her into his arms

again; the moon had risen higher in the sky before he reluctantly let her go.

The drive back to the highway was a hundred times more pleasant than the drive to the beach had been. Kristy was belted into the middle seat, so close her leg touched his and the subtle fragrance of her perfume reached his nose. So this is love, he mused, and realized everything that had come before this had been at best a pale imitation of the real thing.

It took quite a while to find the right dirt road leading to Hank Roscoe's house, as the only time Kristy had been there had been at night and her memory was a little foggy. Booker didn't mind the extra time it took, not one bit.

"That one," Kristy said at last as Booker drove by a road flanked by two old pine trees.

"Are you sure?" he asked. The road was dark; no well-lit house was visible through the trees.

"I should have remembered the pines before. That's the one."

Booker backed up and turned down the road. "I don't think anyone is home," he said as they reached the end of what turned into a narrow driveway and a small, dark house presented itself.

"I'll just knock. If I wake him up, I'll make a joke out of it."

They got out of the truck. It was so dark and silent, Booker decided to leave the headlamps on. Crickets stopped serenading as their feet crunched on the dry pine needles of the path which led to the front porch.

Kristy reached out to knock on the door and was surprised when her touch sent it flying inward.

They looked at each other.

Kristy took a small step inside. "Hank?" she called.

She looked over her shoulder toward Booker. "This is weird," she said.

Booker reached around her and felt for an electrical switch. He flipped it on and said, "Kristy, will you wait here for a second while I look around?"

"Male chauvinist," she said, but he noticed she came inside the room and stayed by the door.

The house was two stories of unfinished pine. Booker noticed half the ceiling was open to rough-hewn beams. He also noticed deep-red leather chairs flanking a fireplace, good rugs on the polished oak floors, and numerous framed photographs of what Booker assumed were Hank's costuming creations for various Cypress Hill Repertory Theater productions framed and hung on the walls. Flipping on light switches as he went, Booker looked into a small kitchen which was as neat as a pin, a small bedroom which looked more a workroom and alternate storage room for the theater than a place to sleep, and a cold bathroom.

Back in the main room, he saw a boxed-in stairway which opened into the dining room around the corner. The stairway must lead upstairs to the master bedroom, he thought. Maybe he'd find Hank sound asleep in his bed.

Booker rounded the corner, but he didn't have to climb the stairs. There on the floor at his feet was the body of Hank Roscoe, and from the looks of things, he'd been dead for a while.

Before Booker could react, he heard a noise behind him. He was too late to stop Kristy from looking down into the vacant eyes of her dead friend.

Chapter Eight

Kristy had finally stopped shaking. Sheriff Fuller was standing off in the corner, talking with Booker. She closed her eyes as the stretcher rattled by, Hank's still form covered with a purple blanket.

How could an evening go from awful, to magical, to horrible all within two hours? She felt completely exhausted and looked up to see if Booker was any closer to getting the sheriff's permission for them to leave.

Both men were approaching her.

"Sorry to see you under these circumstances again so soon, Miss Wilder," the sheriff said. This evening he was dressed in jeans and a battered flannel shirt. Kristy wondered if they'd gotten him out of bed or away from the television.

"I am, too," Kristy said. "Can you tell what happened to Hank?"

"Coroner said a broken neck, looks like a fall, but we'll do an autopsy to make sure. Now, Mr. Booker here tells me you and he heard Roscoe state he had an appointment with someone last night."

"That's right," Kristy said. "The way he said it, I

141

got the feeling he was talking about an engagement with someone, not a business appointment.''

''Do you have any idea who this engagement was with?''

Kristy shook her head. ''None.''

''Because it looks as though,'' the sheriff continued, ''someone picked him up outside the theater last night and brought him home. His truck is still parked outside the theater, is that right?''

''A minivan. Yes, or at least it was when Booker and I left earlier this evening. We were wondering if he had car trouble.''

''We'll check it out. Now, to your knowledge did Roscoe have any enemies?''

Startled at the change in the direction of the questions, Kristy asked, ''Are you suggesting his death wasn't accidental?''

''No, but we like to cover all the bases.''

''Everyone liked Hank,'' Kristy said, thinking of his quick smile and lively sense of humor, to say nothing of the costumes he was able to whip out of a scrap of cloth and thin air. It seemed utterly impossible he was dead. What would the theater do without him?

''He was wonderful,'' she added fondly. ''During the day he worked at a preschool. I heard all the kids adored him. I don't know, Sheriff Fuller. I guess I didn't really know Hank that well outside the theater. I don't have the slightest idea if he had enemies or not. Maybe someone else at the theater might know, but I don't.''

''We'll check with them. Do you know if he had family?''

"I think a mother in Idaho. Maybe his address book—"

"Right. Well, I've got your home and work phone numbers, so as far as I'm concerned, you two are free to leave."

Kristy felt Booker's hand underneath her arm. She nodded at the sheriff, and they escaped into the night, the cold wind drawing icy fingers over their faces.

"Why did the sheriff ask if Hank had any enemies?" Kristy asked as they bumped their way along Hank's dirt road. She was sitting right beside Booker, his leg touching her leg. Given a choice, she'd stayed glued to his side as long as possible.

Booker shook his head, but he glanced down at her quickly. "Did you notice Hank was wearing the same striped shirt he wore last night at rehearsal?"

"No," Kristy said. "I didn't notice his clothes at all." But she could still see his face. She could still see his open eyes—

"Well, I did," Booker said firmly. "The shirt has broad stripes with a little green paisley design running through the middle; it was hardly ordinary."

"I guess he didn't change clothes before he fell," Kristy said. Her head had begun to throb, just as it had after Nancy died.

"But all the lights were off. Think about it. Hank got a ride home with someone, went upstairs for some reason, came back down in the dark and fell."

"Maybe the darkness on the stairs is the reason he fell," Kristy said.

"The stairs are oak, not highly polished, no carpet runner. His clothes were nonobtrusive, and he'd obviously lived in that house for some time. What did he fall on? If he had trouble with the stairs, why didn't he flip on the light? I could see a switch on the wall upstairs, and like the rest of the switches in the house, it was off.''

''I don't know,'' Kristy said. She pushed her fingers against her head and added, ''Wait. Maybe he came downstairs in the daylight, like this morning.''

''If he did, that means he had a fatal slip in broad daylight. Remember, there was nothing in sight on the stairs or beside Hank that he could have tripped over. And it means he didn't change clothes.''

Kristy sighed deeply. ''Is this accident going into the paper?''

''We're right back where we started, back at the beginning after Nancy's death.''

''More or less.''

''Can you think of a reason why it shouldn't be in the paper?'' he asked.

''No,'' she answered quickly and honestly.

For several minutes they traveled in silence; then Booker cleared his throat. ''What do you suppose the ratio of accidental and suicidal deaths is between here and L.A.? Ten to one? A hundred to one? A thousand? And yet I'm here a little over a month, and I'm the first person on the scene after one of each. Two dead people, both young, both healthy. This never happened to me once in Los Angeles, Kristy, not once.''

When he let her off at home, he caught her hand. ''Are you okay?'' he asked.

''My head is splitting open, that's all,'' she told him.

"The oldest excuse in the book," he teased, his eyes concerned. "Would you like me to sleep on your sofa?"

"You go on home to Ida Collins's bed," Kristy said, and they both laughed at the way it sounded.

They shared a lingering kiss, reminding Kristy of the middle of the evening, the part where she'd learned he loved her, the part where her future had fallen into place and reduced her problems to annoyances. Booker's good night was full of promises and sent Kristy to bed with a faint smile on her lips. She slept dreamlessly.

The mail the next afternoon brought a plain white envelope with unfamiliar writing on it. Kristy stared at it for several minutes. There was no return address, and the postmark was so smudged, she couldn't make out where it had originated. The envelope looked exactly like the one James Winterberg had received at the theater twice before; was she now going to find out what it was all about?

Strangely, she felt uneasy about opening the envelope. She put it on the bed as she changed from a work dress to jeans, and still she stared at it. Maybe she should take it to the theater and let Booker open it for her. That thought died immediately; since when did she dodge her own mail and rely on a broad pair of shoulders to ease her mind?

She glanced at her watch and was appalled to discover how much time she'd wasted staring at a white envelope. Dress rehearsal in less than an hour, and she was pacing around the bedroom like a fool. In one quick movement, she snatched up the letter, ripped open the envelope, and unfolded the white piece of paper within.

The results were distinctly anticlimactic as the letter turned out to be from Ida Collins:

Dear Kristy, here is the combination to Nancy's brief-case. Don't know what I was thinking about to leave without giving it to you. I remember it because Nancy joked it was the same as her I.Q., 1–7–7. I don't think she was that smart, or she wouldn't have taken up with that cowboy singer. Anyway, Spokane is nice. Hope your young man is enjoying my furniture. Anne says hi. Yours truly, Ida Collins.

Kristy retrieved the briefcase from her closet and plopped it down on the bed. She spun the tumblers to the right numbers and popped open the lid. Inside lay a script to *Tree Tops* and a stack of other papers Kristy didn't have the time or inclination to read. She closed the lid and with another hurried glance at her watch, left her apartment and drove to the theater.

Another ghost haunted Cypress Hill Repertory Theater, Kristy thought as she hurried in the stage door. However, her sorrow over Hank's death was tempered by the knowledge of what had happened between her and Booker, and her disdain for facing James was similarly tempered by knowing she'd also see the man she loved.

He reached out and took her hand, squeezing it quickly and releasing it. They'd spoken on the phone that afternoon, and Booker had agreed until things were clearer and for reasons of their own, they would act like friends and nothing else when they were around the theater group. Kristy didn't want James taking his obvious dislike for her out on Booker, while Booker confessed he was anxious to find out what had been in those envelopes, and he thought his chances for snooping were better if James didn't know how Booker really felt about Kristy.

It seemed very strange to Kristy to stand on the stage with only Regina as an audience, knowing Hank wasn't upstairs sewing on a lost button or creating a last-minute flounce on a dreary skirt. She looked around at the other faces, all covered with thick makeup emphasizing their characters' traits, and wondered how many of them knew about Hank. Her question was answered when Winterberg strode onto the stage and asked them all to listen to him for a moment; he had an announcement to make.

"By now you all know about Hank Roscoe's fatal accident last night," he said.

Kristy looked swiftly at Booker, but he didn't correct James's timetable, and she certainly wasn't going to.

"We'll all miss Hank," James continued. "Thankfully, purely from a selfish point of view, he'd completed the costumes for *Someday Soon*, and his assistant, Teri Brown, will be able to see us through this production. As for the future? Well, that's for the board to decide. They'll have a devil of a time replacing Hank."

"He was a genius," Summer said softly, and everyone agreed. "It's just awful."

"It might get worse," James warned. "The sheriff

told me he's coming over here tonight during our rehearsal to question everyone about Hank's whereabouts night before last.''

There was a general murmur of alarm. Kristy's gaze met Booker's. She wondered if he was thinking the same thing she was, that the sheriff had drawn some of the same conclusions Booker had the night before.

"Does the sheriff suspect foul play or something?" Duncan Barnett asked.

"That's absurd," Summer said. "Hank was a gentle, sweet man."

Kristy looked out into the audience and saw Regina sitting very still, her eyes glued to her husband's face. Out of nowhere, the thought flickered across Kristy's mind that Regina knew something and it had to do with her husband. She looked away quickly.

"Please, everyone," James said. "Best thing we can do is get through rehearsal before the sheriff comes. Opening night is in a week. I see some of you are already in costume. The rest of you will find yours in the dressing room, so let's be snappy. Oh, and by the way, you'll have an audience tonight."

"On the first dress rehearsal?" Summer asked.

"I know it's unusual, but a class in theater production at the junior college wants to sit in for extra credit. Their assignment is to critique the play, and frankly, I think the outside input will be good for us."

Rona straightened her round shoulders. "I, for one, find an audience exhilarating!"

Kristy smiled when a few eyes turned her way. She didn't feel ready for an audience, but on the other hand, she wasn't sure she ever would. She said, "It should be fun,'' and hoped her words sounded braver than she felt.

"There's only thirty of them," James said. "Let's just hope the sheriff doesn't come while they're still here, or they'll get more than they bargained for."

As Kristy pulled her pink-and-white gown on over her body suit, she was again swamped with memories of Hank. Booker was next to her, buttoning the gray shirt his character wore. He looked to see if anyone was watching, then leaned down and kissed the top of her head. "Break a leg," he whispered.

"Are you nervous about having an audience?" she asked.

"Who, me? Virile macho men like me don't get nervous about a few college kids. Banish the thought!"

"You are, aren't you?"

"Scared to death. Do you need help pinning on that hat?"

"Would you?" She stood very close to him and very still as his fingers manipulated the pins which joined the massive hat to her hair. When he looked at her, his eyes glowed with warmth; the look inflamed Kristy's heart.

Ten minutes into the play, Kristy exited stage center and hurried along the dark corridor, lit only by blue light, to the dressing room which was lit in the same manner. As she took off her coat and hung it up, she heard a noise upstairs. Summer was probably lost in the dark up there, struggling with the tiny buttons which ran down the front of her costume. "You'd better hurry, Summer," she whispered. "There's about fifty people out there."

Just as she looked back toward the rack and put her hands up to unpin the hat, she heard a clanking sound above. Before she could move or look up again, a heavy object hit her on the head. She fell to the floor in a blaze of pain at the same time the falling object clanked down beside her.

Booker was elbow deep in a wheelbarrow of clean, loose soil, busy potting a pink flower of some kind. The flower wasn't real, but he tried to treat it gently just like a man who loved flowers might handle a real one. He kept one eye on the plant and one eye on Rona Duncan. He kept both ears on the dialogue. He only had one line to utter in this whole silly play, and he didn't want to louse it up. Especially in front of a bunch of know-it-all kids who would probably delight in a guffaw of some kind.

He had discovered he wasn't an actor. He didn't like being on the stage, he didn't like listening to the same boring lines night after night, he didn't like people watching him, and he didn't like fooling around in dirt. The only thing he liked about this whole production was being near Kristy, and he liked that so much, it helped get him through the rest of it. He only hoped Rona wouldn't throw herself down to the ground quite so energetically tonight; last night she'd almost taken Kristy down with her.

Rona, as Gloria, the maid, was now arguing with Duncan, who played the part of the Butler, Giles. Duncan handed Rona a shoe box, Rona opened it, supposedly found the dead body of everyone's favorite canary, and screamed. She threw her arm up to her head, turned around a couple of times, and looked at Booker. He knew Kristy was standing right on the other side of the door waiting for his line. He yelled, "Watch out, Miss Gloria!"

Nothing. Kristy had missed her cue. Booker peered into the audience, but the house lights were off, and he couldn't see if Winterberg was in among the sea of faces or not. Not sure what to do, he hollered it again.

Rona, assuming Kristy was there this time, threw herself backward. She fell with a resounding thud. While the rest of the actors—to say nothing of the audience—responded with everything from concern to snickers, Booker stared at the doorway. Where was Kristy?

A premonition washed over him. He scrambled to his feet and, dropping the trowel and the plastic plant, leapt over the fake rock wall and tore open the fragile door. He made his way down the dark hall and burst into the dressing room. A shape lay huddled on the floor, blue light shimmering on white fabric. Booker fell to his knees and cradled Kristy in his arms.

"Kristy love," he whispered, his fingers touching her throat, finding her heartbeat.

"Booker?" she whispered.

"It's all right," he murmured. He heard footsteps and voices. "Turn on a light!" he yelled. A light flickered on.

Kristy's eyes were open, and she was staring at him. The huge hat was tilted down over her right cheek, but enough skin was exposed to show a huge red welt over the entire side of her face.

"What's she doing in here?" Rona hissed. "I made a fool of myself—"

"We need ice," Booker interrupted.

Summer was behind Rona. "There's some in the makeup-room refrigerator," she said quickly and hurried off.

Winterberg pushed Rona aside and kneeled down on the other side of Kristy. He touched her face. Booker needed every ounce of his self-control not to hit the man's hand away.

"What happened to her?" Winterberg asked.

Booker ignored him. He looked up toward the ceiling of the dressing room. "There's another room above this one, isn't there?" Booker asked.

"The women's dressing room," Winterberg said. "No one uses it."

"I used it earlier this evening," Summer said as she returned with a few ice cubes dropped into a knee-high stocking. "It's all I could think of in a hurry," she said quietly.

"It's fine. Get her hat off."

Summer's nimble fingers unpinned the hat. Booker gasped internally when he saw Kristy's beautiful face, swollen and angry. He parted her hair very gently and saw very little swelling. The hat had protected her.

"Look around for something heavy," Booker said.

Winterberg said, "Why?"

Was the man an idiot? Booker said, "Because something fell from up there and hit her."

Summer lifted the hem of Kristy's dress. She held up a fourteen-inch pipe wrench. Booker knew they weighed in at around eight pounds. Falling six or seven feet, the thing might easily have killed anyone standing beneath it.

"That's the missing pipe wrench," Winterberg said. "Why would a workman leave it up there?"

"It wasn't up there earlier tonight," Summer said.

Booker looked at her. "You're sure?"

"Positive."

Booker's mind reeled as he realized someone must have taken it up later; someone must have pushed it through one of the cracks in the ceiling. Suddenly it seemed very important to get Kristy out of the theater. She hadn't spoken since saying his name, but he had the distinct impression it was because she was too busy listening. "I'm taking you to the hospital," he told her.

"Good," she whispered. "My head hurts."

He looked at Summer. "Pick that pipe wrench up with your skirt and put it in a brown paper bag, will you? When the sheriff comes, tell him what happened and give him the bag."

"Wait a second," Winterberg said. "You're not in charge in this theater."

"James, we have an audience," Rona said. "What are we going to do?"

Winterberg stared at Kristy and Booker, his managerial ego at war with pride of his play. Pride won. "We'll keep going. Summer, do you know Kristy's part?"

"Well, sure, but—"

"Okay, I'll make an announcement, and we'll start over again. You play Lydia. Rona, do you know the part of Anna Thorton?"

"I know every brilliant word you wrote, James. I have memorized every line, every—"

"Fine, fine. We'll write out Gloria; it's a small part, anyway. This is how we'll handle it."

Booker ignored the rest. He stood, Kristy in his arms, her hands clasping his shoulders, and he smiled down into her face.

"You don't have to carry me," she said softly. "I can walk."

"Don't ruin this terribly gallant gesture, please," he said with a grin. When he looked at the others who were now watching him, he found speculation in Winterberg's eyes. "You'll have to do without the gardener, too," he said and left them as they once again began working out how they'd get through the performance, which was really only supposed to be a dress rehearsal. The fear in Booker's heart was that the episode with the pipe wrench had been another kind of dress rehearsal and that the real performance might conclude with Kristy dead.

Sheriff Fuller caught up with them as the doctor finished examining Kristy's face. "Ice pack and aspirin," the doctor said and discreetly left the room.

"Well, now," Sheriff Fuller said. This time he was wearing his green uniform, complete with badge and handcuffs. "You're going to have a heck of a bruise there in a few days," he added.

"Did Summer Sanders give you the pipe wrench?" Booker asked.

"It's out in the car. Of course, people know better

than to leave their fingerprints on anything nowadays. Only ones we'll find will be Miss Sanders's.''

"Summer's!" Kristy cried.

"She picked it up," Booker told her.

"Now you tell me what happened," the sheriff said calmly.

As Kristy told her story, she was aware of a knot forming in Booker's jaw. The sheriff, on the other hand, showed no response to her tale.

"Only trouble is," he said, "these old buildings are full of noises. And it's almost impossible to pin down the exact location of anyone who wasn't on the stage because of all those students." He seemed very interested in the fact that Summer was the only one to use the upstairs dressing room.

"But she wouldn't hurt me. I mean, what would be her motive?"

"She was doing a grand job in your part tonight," the sheriff said, a hint of speculation in his voice.

"Sheriff, this is hardly Broadway. We don't even ⌐ money for running back and forth to the theater. ⌐ a woman try to kill another woman for a ⌐more lines? It's ridiculous.''

⌐ttered, "But you didn't die, did ⌐at you're unable to perform ⌐lace.''

⌐ certainty.

⌐ Booker asked.

⌐ to Booker. "Are you ⌐are connected?''

⌐dences," Booker said.

⌐ed to talk to him in front

of several people. The next day he turns up dead, and the day after that she's almost killed."

"It was an accident," Kristy said wearily. It was too preposterous to think anyone would really want to harm her. But the resolute steeliness of Booker's expression as the sheriff said the autopsy results would take another day warned Kristy the matter was far from over.

Who hated her enough to kill her? The only one she could think of was James Winterberg, and she wasn't sure he really hated her, and if he did, she had no idea why. Was Summer possibly envious enough to try to injure Kristy hoping—no, knowing—she'd be given the lead? No. Could she be so angry with Kristy for getting the part she knew should have been hers that she'd—No, Kristy decided. A hundred times no.

Kristy made it to school the next day, though a quick look in the mirror halfway through the day convinced her she should have listened to Booker and the doctor and taken the day off. By fourth period it felt as though a percussion band were giving a concert inside her head. She made it through the afternoon, then drove herself home and put herself to bed with another i pack. Dress rehearsal in less than three hours, an nap sounded like a slice of heaven.

She slept fitfully for an hour until the phon her. "It's me," Booker announced when swered. "How are you?"

"Fine," she said, struggling to sound wouldn't start worrying about her again of being in his arms, of looking up at h her to his car, of feeling like the most precious prize in the world to a man like him overwhelmed her, and she felt her throat close.

"I wish you'd stay home tonight," he said.

"I have to go," she told him. "Remember, there was no dress rehearsal last night, and opening night is so soon it scares me. I can't let the cast down."

"But Summer could cover for you—"

"Like she did last night. I know she could, but that means Rona takes the part of Anna Thorton and slaughters the play. I know that sounds mean, but you know what Rona is like. Besides, my family is coming for the opening-night performance, and I don't want to disappoint them."

"They'd be more disappointed if the next time a pipe wrench falls, you don't happen to have an oversized hat on your head."

"It was an accident, Booker. No, don't say anything, I don't want to argue with you. By the way, has it occurred to you that Hank may have saved my life by creating that hat?"

"Yes," he said, his voice husky. "Kristy, if anything happens to you, I don't know what I'll do."

"Nothing is going to happen to me," she assured him. "I'll see you tonight."

"Take it easy until then," he cautioned.

"I'm in bed. I have Nancy's briefcase to go through and your newspaper to read. I can hardly wait to see what Addie has to say this week."

"Don't remind me. I have a stack of irate mail on my desk about my advice to dump the smelly hubby out in the sea."

"Ah, life at the top. Good-bye. I love you."

"Kristy? Wait a moment. I want to tell you about my name."

"The mysterious initials? Not on your life. I don't want news like that over the phone. See you later."

Kristy smiled as she recradled the phone. This being-in-love stuff was really wonderful, she mused as she opened the paper. She found the Ask Addie column and laughed as she read Booker's advice to the woman who was sick of sitting in the backseat while her husband's mother sat in the front seat beside her son on their weekly jaunts to and from church.

Give the old lady a break, he wrote, *and hope your son gives you one someday, too.*

The *Cypress Tribune* was a small newspaper, and within half an hour Kristy had read it cover to cover. Next week there'd be an article in the paper about Hank Roscoe's death. She hoped the autopsy showed some natural reason why Hank may have toppled down those stairs, like a heart attack or something. The worry and suspicion of the last few days were getting on Kristy's nerves.

She refolded the newspaper and spied the briefcase. Holding the mostly melted ice pack to her face, she retrieved the case and climbed back in bed. The combination was easy to remember—she just thought of Nancy's supposed I.Q., 1–7–7. She lifted out Nancy's copy of the script to *Tree Tops* and looked through it, fond memories resurfacing like bubbles from the bottom of a champagne glass. After some time she set that aside and looked at the other papers in the case. What she found made her sit up straighter.

How could Nancy have had a complete script for *Someday Soon* before *Tree Tops* was even finished? James Winterberg hadn't passed them out until well after Nancy's suicide. Kristy read the familiar words—there was no doubt.

Was it really the same? She decided to read it from beginning to end. By the time she got to the last two pages, her mouth was dry and her heart was beating like the wings of a moth caught in a glass jar.

She picked up the phone and called Booker at the newspaper office. His secretary, Janet, answered the phone.

"Mr. Booker told me you might call. He said to tell you he was going to the harbor to talk to a fisherman named Tom Jones about an article he wants to do on the local fishing situation. After that he's going to the theater. Would you like to leave a message?"

"If he calls you, tell him to get in touch with me right away," Kristy said. "It's urgent."

"Will do," Janet said.

This time Kristy hung up the phone with a frown creasing her forehead. She looked at her alarm clock. It was time to get ready to go to the theater. She put the typewritten script for *Someday Soon* back in the briefcase and locked it. She'd take it to the theater with her. Maybe she was reading too much into it, but suddenly certain things looked very suspicious, while other things turned into darker mysteries than they'd been before. She wasn't sure enough to call Sheriff Fuller without running it by Booker's facile mind first, but she started to think she'd better start guarding her back.

Kristy was one of the first to arrive. She put on her makeup quickly while Summer fussed over her and asked if Kristy was sure she was "up to this." Kristy assured her she was.

"I was awful as Lydia," Summer said as she swept her hair into a French twist. She leaned closer and added, "And Rona Barnett made the prim Anna Thorton into a sleazy dance-hall girl. It was actually funny. And you should have heard the critiques we got from the kids in the theater-production class! And then the sheriff was here asking all sorts of questions about Hank Roscoe and then about you . . . . Well, Kristy, you missed the most exciting night in this theater in years."

James came through the door right then, and Summer turned back to her makeup. He was followed by Rona and the rest of the cast, all except Booker, that is. Kristy was very aware of the time bomb she might be carrying around in Nancy's briefcase. It was on the counter in front of her; she wished she'd left it in her car, but she'd been so sure Booker would be early and they'd have a chance to talk.

"Your face looks fine," James said to Kristy, his eyes and voice so guarded it was impossible to tell how he really felt.

She nodded. "This makeup could cover anything."

"And you're sure you're well enough to perform tonight?"

"Yes," she said. Out of the corner of her eye, she could see how disappointed Rona was to hear this piece of news. Rona came closer and peered into the mirror at Kristy's reflection. "Are you sure?" she asked hopefully.

"Positive. I just hope the workmen haven't left any more tools lying around."

"I had Jack Osborne check upstairs," James said.

Rona suddenly said, "Is that Nancy's briefcase? It is, isn't it? I recognize the leather. What are you doing with it?"

Kristy sighed. Struggling to be polite, she said, "Nancy's mom gave it to me." She looked at all the familiar faces turned her way and felt like Benedict Arnold for suspecting what she did.

Just then Booker waltzed into the makeup room. James looked at his watch and announced, "You're late."

"I'm sorry," Booker said. "My makeup is easy, you know. A little smudge here, a dirt clod there."

James frowned, but he left the room. "I want Kristy and Todd out now for a small change in the blocking," he said from the doorway. "The rest of you have ten minutes."

Kristy leaned down over Booker's shoulder as she passed him. "I have to talk to you," she said. She smelled the faint aroma of whiskey on his breath—he and Tom Jones had apparently been at it again, though obviously not to the same extent as the first time.

"I want to talk to you, too," he said. "Are you sure you're okay?"

"I'm fine."

He narrowed his eyes. "Just watch your head," he warned and then added, "Later, I want to run a story idea by that pretty head of yours."

Kristy nodded, but she didn't have time to stay. She did take time to run out to her car and lock the briefcase into the trunk, but talking with Booker about her suspicions would have to wait until after rehearsal.

This time they were back to playing to an audience of one, Regina Winterberg. Kristy looked at her friend before the house lights went off and wondered if Regina would ever forgive her, if she was right, for what she going to do. Probably not. In her heart, guilt warred with morality, and neither won.

This time things went off without a hitch. Kristy delivered her last spunky line and the curtain went down, just like it would on opening night if there was an opening night. While James gave yet more directions, Kristy stole a look at Booker, who winked at her. That story he was following must be a doozy, she thought.

"Tom Jones is a real salt-of-the-earth type of guy," Booker told Kristy as they lingered on the stage after James had offered the last suggestion for improving each actor's performance.

"I believe you told me that once before," she said.

He laughed. "It's good to be writing a story about something that matters, Kristy love. All this undefined mystery around the theater has been more frustrating than I figured, I guess, because today when I was out there interviewing a few of the guys, getting a story with all sorts of government involvement, I felt my little reporter's heart go pitter-patter."

"Pitter-patter, huh?" Kristy repeated fondly.

"This can wait. You wanted to talk to me about something?"

Kristy said, "Let's go sit in the audience for a moment, and you tell me your story first. There's time for my . . . discovery." As they took two seats, Kristy thought how much she loved him, how wonderful it was to listen to his ideas. In a few minutes she'd show him what was in the briefcase, and if she was right, he'd get the biggest story to hit Cypress Hill in years. For this one minute she wanted him to enjoy the story he was researching on his own.

"It'll be a human-interest piece," Booker said, finishing his tale. "That's what the *Tribune* has been lacking. I want to give the paper more breadth, make it reflect this community. Okay, now it's your turn."

They both looked up when they heard footsteps on the stage. "Listen, you two," Jack Osborne said. "You've been chatting out there for the better part of an hour. We'd like to go home."

Booker laughed. "Sorry, Jack. Come on, Kristy, let's get out of here."

They changed back into street clothes and went outside. Besides Jack's old blue truck, their cars were the only two left in the dimly lit parking lot.

"I found something in Nancy's briefcase," Kristy said as she took out her key and prepared to open the trunk.

"I hope you didn't leave it back here," Booker said. "Your lock has been jimmied open." As he lifted the trunk hood, Kristy peered over his shoulder.

"It's gone," she moaned. "I'm stupid and dumb, and it's gone."

"What's gone?"

"Proof, Booker. Proof Nancy didn't kill herself. And like a fool, I took it into the theater."

"What are you talking about?"

"Nancy's briefcase."

"Maybe we should go somewhere and talk," Booker said after a lengthy pause.

Kristy nodded.

"And let's take my car. Leave yours here, just in case it was tampered with."

"You don't think—"

"I don't know what to think," he said seriously. "Let's go."

Chapter Nine

" "Feel better?"

Kristy took the towel off her hair and felt the curly wet strands fall against her neck. "Much," she said. She'd used Booker's shower to wash off the makeup. While she'd dressed again, he'd showered and put on sweatpants and a sweatshirt. He looked wonderfully cuddly in the informal clothes, and Kristy sat down next to him on the sofa.

"I built a fire so your hair would dry," he said. He ran gentle fingers down the left side of Kristy's face. She knew it looked sore and still a little puffy. To her relief, he didn't say anything about it.

"Are you ready to tell me about the briefcase now?" he asked.

Kristy nodded. For a few moments, sitting next to him, with the fire blazing a few feet away and light dancing on the walls, she'd managed to put aside the unease she'd felt since discovering her trunk lock broken and the briefcase gone. It came back now with a rush, and she shivered. Slowly, in detail, she told him about finding the script to *Someday Soon*.

165

"Maybe he just gave her an advance copy," Booker said.

"The script is not exactly the same," Kristy explained. "This one has a better ending."

"Then why do you suppose he changed it? The ending he has now stinks."

"Do you think so, too? I've always wondered why he didn't have Lydia do anything. Now I know. Originally, he did. When she discovers Fenton doesn't love her, that he really covets Anna Thorton, she jumps off a cliff."

"The Anna Thorton part is good, only what cliff?"

"The play in the briefcase takes place in Greece, not England, on a patio overlooking the Mediterranean sea, not in a garden with a gazebo. And the characters' names are all changed. Fenton's name is Tom in this version. *Tom*, Booker. He's a rich visiting American. That doesn't matter. What matters are the words the character cries before she does herself in. I'll use the names we're familiar with. Lydia says, 'There is no meaning.' Anna Thorton says, 'Yes.' Then Lydia says, 'I mean it. You've been a friend, and I appreciate it, but it's not enough. You don't understand. Fenton is lost to me now, and I won't go on, I just won't. You can't make me.' "

Booker whistled through his teeth. "Are those like the words you heard Nancy say?"

"Booker, I'd swear they're exactly the same words! Only remember, in the play I found, Lydia says, 'Tom is lost to me now, etc.' *Tom*."

"And the rest of it?"

"Every word I remember Nancy saying, every single

word. And at the last, when she screams, 'I can't go on, I just can't,' James has her up on a wall which surrounds the patio, and he has her jump. That's the ending he wrote for the play. I think that's the ending Nancy was performing for him the night she died.''

''He must have convinced Nancy to try out that night at his house, promising her the lead, plotting her murder.''

''I think so. The pages in the briefcase were copies. I think she made a copy of the script he gave her because I'm sure he demanded the original back, swore her to secrecy. When he saw that case tonight, it must have scared the daylights out of him. He must have wondered if she'd double-crossed him, so he broke into my car and stole the case.''

Booker swore under his breath. ''When he opens the case and finds the original script, he'll guess you've read it, Kristy.''

She threw herself to her feet and stood in front of the huge fireplace. She was shivering so hard, her voice rattled. ''So many things now make sense, Booker. Nancy wasn't drunk downstairs; she was acting. But upstairs, before the police came, I saw two brandy snifters. What if he got her drunk up there? That's something else I forgot to tell you. The character in the play is drinking ouzo while she threatens to end her life. I think he had Nancy drinking brandy. By the time the sheriff came, the glasses were gone. No one thought to really search the place because we'd all heard Nancy ranting and raving. We'd all heard her verbal suicide note.''

''But why?'' Booker asked. ''Why would he go to

all the risk of plotting this bizarre murder to kill Nancy Collins?''

"Think about it this way: Nancy told everyone at the theater she had a new boyfriend, but she wouldn't tell a soul who he was. That wasn't like Nancy, trust me. She didn't mention Charlie Hook to any of us. She never mentioned a name. What if it was James Winterberg? What if she just used Charlie Hook to mislead her mother? And what if she was threatening to tell Regina about their affair?''

Booker nodded. "So to shut her up he plots to kill her. He gives her his play and says she can have a private audition the night of the cast party. Then he tells her to put on a big scene downstairs so the two of them have fifteen minutes alone upstairs while Rona and Duncan sing. It doesn't make sense to audition like this, but Nancy is too excited to care about details, and James wants a large audience for her parting words.''

"So," Kristy continued, "James fixes the door so it won't open. Nancy says her lines, James reading the part of Anna Thorton. Only at the last, when he has her out on the balcony, drunk as the proverbial skunk on brandy, he pushes her. Then I come into the room. The first thing he asked me was if I'd seen what happened. Of course, I hadn't. He acts all contrite and sad, and we all believe him. He even repeats some of her words and tells us it's his playwright's memory!''

Booker got to his feet and came to Kristy. He took her hands. "This doesn't explain the pipe wrench, and it doesn't explain Hank Roscoe.''

"I know," she said. "Except that Hank said some

rumors about Nancy were true and some weren't. What if James started all the rumors about Nancy being a drunk and about her suicidal tendencies just to pave the road for Nancy's 'suicide'? Maybe Hank knew or suspected.''

"So maybe Winterberg killed Hank. But why in the world would he want to kill you?"

"I haven't the slightest idea," Kristy said.

"We're calling the sheriff," Booker said.

Kristy only nodded. She stared into the flames and thought about Hank's words. "Theater is illusion," he'd said. So were some people, Kristy mused.

Booker didn't like this one bit. He looked at the sheriff and Kristy deep in conversation and shook his head. No, he didn't like this.

Okay, he would admit the evidence against Winterberg, in other words, the original version of *Someday Soon*, was gone. By now it was most likely a pile of ashes in Winterberg's fireplace. Nancy Collins's body had been cremated, so if there'd been any clues there, it was too late now. All they had was Kristy's word that *Someday Soon* first existed in another form. There was always the selection committee, but were they likely to go against a man like Winterberg on the strength of their memories?

The sheriff had already gotten the office administrator out of her bed to check the records. Booker hadn't been surprised to hear the copy on file was the same as the copy presently being produced. Winterberg would have had ample opportunity to replace the original copy with one of the new ones—there was no security in the office at the theater. Why should there be?

Besides, who was to say Winterberg was lying if he said he'd been uncomfortable with the similarities between his play and Nancy's death and so rewrote it?

However, he still didn't like the plot Fuller and Kristy were busy hatching. It put Kristy in a lot of danger, and it could backfire. He'd watch her every minute, he decided. Karen and Frank could work on the newspaper. He was going to work on keeping Kristy alive.

She stayed at his house that night. He knew she wouldn't have if the sheriff hadn't agreed it was a smart thing to do. Booker made her take his bed; then he settled down on the couch, alone, with a blanket and warm desires to hold Kristy in his arms. It was at the moment his eyes finally closed for the night that he made the decision to ask her to marry him.

"About my name," he said as he drove her to her house the next morning.

"The mysterious initials A.W. Are you finally going to tell me what they stand for?"

"Brace yourself. I want to know how you feel about becoming Mrs. Aldous Wilbur Booker?" He felt Kristy staring at him. He sneaked a look and said, "Which part has you speechless, the name or the marriage proposal?"

"Both," she said at last. "The name is a little bit of a disappointment," she added after a few seconds' thought. "I don't know what I was expecting, but it was worse than Aldous Wilbur."

"Will you marry me?" Booker asked, glad he was

able to pull to the curb in front of her house so he could look at her.

She was staring at her lap. "I love you," she said. "There's no doubt at all about that."

"Then why do you hesitate?"

She looked at him. "Because you married hastily once before. Don't you think we should give ourselves the summer?"

"I won't make it through a summer."

"Sure you will," she said.

Booker got out of the car and went around to open Kristy's door. When she got to her feet, he swooped her into his arms and kissed her soundly. "I won't last the summer," he repeated, looking deep into her eyes. "And I'm going to keep kissing you like that until you won't last, either."

"What a threat!" Kristy said.

He walked her to her door, looked around her house, went back to his car. After she changed clothes, he was going to drive her to school. After school he was going to pick her up and bring her back here until time for the last rehearsal *Someday Soon* would ever have. Only this time, the play was going to be different. This time it was being performed by the late Nancy Collins.

"What do you think?" Kristy asked. It was an hour before rehearsal started. Booker had spent the last few hours hoping the sheriff's end of things was going well, and if it wasn't, that the man would have the brains to talk Kristy out of her scheme to bring James Winterberg to justice.

Now he looked at the woman he loved and felt his jaw drop. "You look just like her," he said.

Kristy nodded, obviously pleased with herself. "I used a hair straightener," she said, fingering the long fall of straight blond hair that now crowned her head. She'd applied stage makeup to make her nose appear a little longer, like Nancy's nose, and colored contact lenses to darken her eyes a few shades. The bruise on the side of her face was covered, and she was wearing deep-red lipstick. She was wearing heels to make her appear another two inches taller, and she was wearing a white dress Booker had watched her buy just for this special performance. It was an eerie-looking long dress that floated around her legs.

"It's spooky," he said.

Kristy nodded nervously. "Well, you only saw her once. Fooling James Winterberg might be harder as he knew her much better. I've even tried to mimic her voice, though. What do you think?"

Booker felt like screaming. He laughed. "I repeat, it's spooky." He paused and added, "I have an idea, though. I happen to know Charlie Hook is at the Lonesome Tortoise. Let's leave now and run you by him. I'd feel a lot better about this if I was sure you looked like Nancy to someone who knew her."

To his relief, Kristy nodded. "Let's hurry then. I don't want to be late."

It had been a cruel idea, Booker decided as he caught sight of Charlie Hook's face when Kristy walked through the door of the Lonesome Tortoise. Booker hadn't meant to be cruel. In fact, he'd hoped Charlie might dissuade Kristy from going through with this.

Instead, Charlie called out Nancy's name, and it took several moments of intense conversation between him and Kristy to get the man back to normal.

"It's going to be okay," Kristy assured Booker once they were back in the car.

He cast her a quick glance, but the sight of her didn't help; she didn't look like herself. "I miss your curls," he said, fully aware it was a selfish and stupid thing to say.

But she smiled at him and patted his leg. "Sheriff Fuller will be there. You'll be there. A deputy will be there. The stage door will be locked and barred so James will have to come in the front door. When he walks down the aisle, the lights will go on. I'll be up on stage. James, hopefully, will spend an uncomfortable minute wondering if Nancy has come back to haunt him. We'll have a tape recorder standing by, and everything he says will be recorded."

"I know all this," Booker said testily, "but why should he spill his guts to you?"

"Because he'll come tonight expecting the whole cast, worrying about the briefcase and what I know and whom I've told. The theater will appear empty, and he'll get even more worried. After all, he's the director. Who would dare to cancel a rehearsal a few days before opening without his consent? The lights will go on, and there I'll be. Hopefully, by then he'll be coming a little unglued. Besides, even if he doesn't for a second think I'm Nancy, even if he realizes exactly who I am, he'll want to shut me up because I obviously know too much. That'll work, too, though

I have to admit, I'd love to worm a confession out of him.''

Booker slammed on the brakes and turned to face her. ''Good heavens, Kristy, we're talking about confronting a murderer here, not a day in the woods with Peter Rabbit. Don't make the man angry. Don't get yourself hurt. Don't—''

''Why do you suppose I didn't say yes this morning when you asked me to marry you?'' Kristy interrupted.

Booker shook his head. ''You said you wanted the summer—''

''Because of tonight. This is something I have to do, Booker. Tonight, while I'm still officially unattached, I can risk what I have to risk to do what I have to do. Tomorrow, after I tell you I want to marry you, I'll have to be more considerate of your feelings. Now, love of my life, please get going because there are two cars honking their horns behind you and I can't be late.''

It had turned out to be just as spooky as he'd feared it would be, and that was a fact. Booker stood off to the side of the stage, hidden by the curtain. Fuller and his cohorts had done a pretty good job of transforming the English garden into a set out of a nightmare. They'd shipped in a fog machine from somewhere, and set up a fan so that the stage was covered with swirling masses of gray mist. Downstage left, diagonal to the gazebo, stood Kristy, only it didn't look like Kristy; it looked like Nancy. In the dim light, her face was pale and heavily shadowed, her dress blended into the mist.

Everything was ready except Booker's heart, which seemed to be lodged somewhere in his right foot.

They waited. It was too dark to see his watch, so he didn't know if the minutes were really crawling by or only seemed to. Booker decided to go behind the scenes and cross over to where he knew Sheriff Fuller was watching. He moved very quickly and very quietly.

He was almost to the sheriff's position when he heard a noise from the audience area. He stood still, held his breath, and dared a peek from behind a fold of curtain. As he did, the lights came on, and the stage seemed to float above a sea of gray mist, Kristy a lone figure pacing back and forth. Out in the audience Booker heard a gasp.

"Who's up there?" Winterberg's voice rang out.

Booker saw Kristy stand very still. She said, "You know who I am, James."

Winterberg came closer. Booker could see him now. His mask of civility was gone.

"You killed me," Kristy said.

Booker was having a hard time remembering this was Kristy and not Nancy's ghost. The woman on the stage didn't look like his Kristy or sound like her or even move like her. He looked toward the spot he was sure Sheriff Fuller should be and saw a dark shape. He took a silent, cautious step in that direction. Onstage, Kristy said, "After all we meant to each other, you killed me. James, how could you have pushed me from that balcony? I loved you."

"Who are you?" Winterberg repeated, his voice a hoarse whisper.

"I'm Nancy, your beloved. I trusted you. But I won't give up my part in your play, James. I'll be Lydia forever. You can be Tom. Come to me, Tom."

She reached out her arms, beckoning. Booker felt his throat go dry when he saw Winterberg begin to climb onto the stage. This wasn't in the script. Booker took another step toward Sheriff Fuller and ran into something on the ground. He knelt down and felt with his hands. As his fingers ran over a human form and connected with something cool and hard, he realized it was the badge on Fuller's chest. Before he could determine if the man was alive or dead, a shape detached itself from the shadows, and his head exploded in a chasm of pain. He slumped over the sheriff's still body.

Kristy's arms were trembling. *Admit it,* she thought, *you're scared to death.* She hadn't expected Winterberg to come up onto the stage with her. She supposed it didn't matter as Sheriff Fuller and Booker were both watching. Remembering to pitch her voice higher, she said, "Tom. Forever and ever together. I'll take you with me—"

"Who are you? What are you doing here? Where is everyone?"

"We don't need anyone else," Kristy said. "I kept your secrets; I didn't tell a soul about us. And I was good as Lydia, wasn't I, Tom? I did what you asked?"

"Who are you?" James whispered in such a way that Kristy's spine tingled with alarm. "You can't be Nancy. You can't know . . . ."

"That you killed me?"

He was silent for such a long time that Kristy began to think the whole idea was a fiasco. Then he cleared his throat and asked, "Who put you up to this? How do you know?"

"About Nancy? About you killing her? Because I am her, James. You can't kill me."

"I already did," he said, his voice loud and clear.

Bingo! Kristy thought, satisfaction chasing fear away. How much more did the sheriff want? She said, "We're lovers in eternity. Nothing you can do can change that."

"I pushed you," he hissed, then shook his head. "I mean, her. I pushed Nancy. I killed her. Do you think I'd let her tell my wife about us? Do you think I'd let her rob me of everything I'd worked so hard to get?"

Enough is enough, Kristy thought. *Come on, Sheriff. Booker?*

"I'll kill again if I have to," James said, and Kristy saw clutched in his hand what she hadn't seen before.

"You can't shoot a ghost," she whispered, backing away from him. "You're no ghost," James said as he raised the gun. "You're Kristy Wilder; you have to be. You look like Nancy, you even sound like her, and now you're going to die like her, too."

Kristy looked frantically toward the sides of the stage. She couldn't see the sheriff or Booker. Where in heaven's name were they? Well, she wasn't going to die up here by herself. She used her own voice and said, "It's over, James. The sheriff is here. He's heard every word you've said."

He didn't seem to hear her. His head was tilted slightly to the left, his eyes wild, as though he weren't sure who he was confronting, as though it didn't matter. He'd killed before, and he was poised to kill again. He shook his head and raised the gun. It exploded as Kristy began to turn away. Winterberg fell to the stage, swallowed by mist. Reeling with fright, Kristy realized he'd been shot, not her.

What had happened? Had the sheriff finally come to her rescue? She walked toward James's body and knelt in the mist. She touched his chest; her fingers came away warm and sticky. She didn't know she'd cried out until another voice drifted through the fog.

"I wouldn't mourn for him if I were you."

Kristy looked toward the voice, utterly confused. "Regina?"

Regina materialized out of the mists from behind the gazebo. "You do look like Nancy, don't you? I was even confused for a moment. Is my dear husband dead?"

"I think so. Sheriff Fuller must have shot him—"

Regina threw back her head and laughed. She raised her hand, and Kristy saw a gun gripped tightly in her fingers.

"You?" Kristy asked.

"He was going to kill you," Regina said. "I should have let him; it would have made everything much easier."

Kristy took a faltering step forward. "I don't understand," she repeated. She looked beyond Regina and called, "Booker? Sheriff Fuller?"

"Along with the deputy in the lighting booth, they're both dead to the world," Regina said. "You'll be joining them soon. Get James's gun and hand it over."

Kristy stopped moving. Utterly bewildered, she mumbled, "Why? What's going on?"

"Get the gun," Regina snapped. She pointed her gun at Kristy's forehead. "Now," she added ominously.

Kristy retrieved the gun still clutched in James's dead hand. She turned it on Regina and said, "I guess it's a stand-off, isn't it?"

"Not really," Regina said smugly. "I put blanks in his gun when I first started blackmailing him. Or, as he believed, you first started blackmailing him."

Kristy blinked rapidly, her mind covering ground at breakneck speed. "You sent him blackmail notes, and you made him think they came from me."

"Oh, little teacher, you get an A +. You weren't the first in James's study the night he killed Nancy Collins. I was. I came in through the bedroom door. He'd locked it, you see, but I had a key."

Kristy nodded, suddenly remembering the noise she'd heard off to her left, the noise she'd dismissed.

"I was in time to see him help Nancy over that railing," Regina said. "I'd known about their affair for weeks, of course, but when I saw him kill her, I knew he was losing it, and if he lost it, so would I. So I kept quiet and started blackmailing him to get every cent I could from his private bank accounts before he ended up dead or in prison."

"But why did you use me?" Kristy pleaded.

Regina shrugged. "You were the first one into the room, and he was never sure you hadn't seen something suspicious. He accepted that the blackmail notes were coming from you right away, just as I knew he would.

In your first note, you demanded the lead in his play and a part for that newspaper reporter you were so friendly with. I thought that was a nice touch and, after all, we were friends. And you also demanded a lot of money.

"Oh, Kristy, it was so great when you showed up in that silly fur coat, waving that humongous diamond around! James about died. And then you demanded even more money, and sure enough, he withdrew it and left it where you said to, but he began to get very nervous. That's when he tried to do away with you by stealing the pipe wrench and dropping it on your head. He never was very good at physical things, however. He bungled the job."

"Why did he kill Hank Roscoe?" Kristy asked. She tried not to think about Booker and Fuller dead. Regina hadn't said they were dead, just that they were dead to the world. *Wake up!* she screamed internally.

"James didn't kill Hank—I did!" Regina said. "I propositioned him, gave him a ride to his house, drugged his wine, and pushed him down his stairs. It was easy. Besides, I had to do it. I heard him talking to you and Rona in the costume room. I knew he was going to tell you about Nancy and James, and from there I knew you'd figure out the rest."

"They're doing an autopsy," Kristy said through clattering teeth. "They'll discover Hank was drugged—"

"And they'll think James killed him. And when they find you here with a gun in your hand, the bullet of which killed poor James, and him with a gun in his hand with a bullet missing that killed you, well, I'll be the poor, grieving widow. The poor, grieving, rich widow.''

''But why did you have to kill him?'' Kristy asked. ''He was your husband—''

''He was everything I loathe in a man. He was weak in spirit and in the flesh. He used me. And last night when he came home with Nancy's briefcase, which he gave her, by the way, as though a briefcase could make something out of that . . . that tramp, his eyes were darting back and forth as though the law were breathing down his neck. That's when I knew I had to get rid of him. It's okay, though. I've got just about everything he secreted away from me.''

For a moment Kristy forgot to be afraid. ''There never was a baby, was there?'' she asked furiously.

Regina smiled. ''You're wrong, there is a baby. Funny, James always wanted children, but I didn't. I've gotten used to the idea now, though. Motherhood will be easier in the south of France with a nanny, don't you think?''

Kristy looked at the gun in her hand. Was it full of blanks or not? Could she risk killing the innocent life Regina carried? In a split second she decided it was a risk she'd have to take. She aimed the gun low and fired at Regina's leg. A loud crash filled the air, but nothing else happened.

Regina walked up to Kristy. ''Give me the gun or I walk back to where your boyfriend is collapsed and kill him before I kill you.''

Kristy handed her the gun and watched as Regina took out the blanks and put in live bullets. She'd always thought she could handle any situation, but she honestly didn't know what to do about this one. If she tried to get lost in the fog, she knew Regina would simply go to the spot she'd left Booker and kill him. She wouldn't trade her life for his. "Just don't hurt Booker," she said.

"Oh, I wouldn't think of it. He and the sheriff will be handy witnesses. I'll just erase some of that tape you said you were making, and it'll sound like you and James killed each other at the same time." She backed up toward the gazebo, and for the second time that night, Kristy looked down the barrel of a gun. She was too afraid to move, too afraid to think. One emotion surfaced: profound regret for the years she and Booker wouldn't have.

"You were the first one in the room," Regina repeated. "It had to be you."

Kristy closed her eyes. But instead of the expected gunshot, she heard a thud and a scuffle. She opened her eyes to see two bodies struggling in the mist. The gun went off. Kristy ran to the scene of the melee just as Booker pushed himself to his feet, the gun in his hand. They looked at each other; then Kristy crashed into his broad chest, and he held her so tightly it crushed her ribs. She didn't mind, not at all.

Eventually she tore herself away. "Is Regina . . . is she dead?"

"The gun discharged into the air. She's out like a light because I punched her in the jaw. Not very gentlemanly of me, but she'll be okay," he said as he pulled Kristy back into his arms.

Sheriff Fuller staggered out onto the stage a moment later and stared at them. "Someone knocked me out," he said. "I saw Winterberg come into the theater, but then someone conked me on the head."

"Regina Winterberg," Booker said. "She must have come into the theater with her husband, only she sneaked around the edges while we were all busy watching him. I didn't hear most of what she said because she knocked me out, too, but I do know she killed Hank Roscoe."

"She killed James, too," Kristy said wearily. "His body is buried in the fog over there. It's all on tape. Sheriff, I want to go home."

The sheriff smiled at her. "You go ahead. I'll catch up with you later."

"And you'd better go check your lighting man," she added as Booker took her hand. "And Regina is pregnant, so you might want to get her to a doctor."

The sheriff took Regina's gun from Booker; then he handcuffed the still unconscious Regina to the gazebo and got to his feet. "I'll take care of all of this. You go home."

"Thank you," Kristy said.

"For what? For almost getting you killed?"

Kristy and Booker laughed softly as they left the theater. Kristy took in a deep lungful of clean salt-tinged air and smiled. For a while there she'd thought she'd never take another breath of fresh air. She'd thought her last breath would be artificial fog and she'd be lost in the swirling gray mist. . . .

" . . . so we'll get married right away," Booker was saying, "and live happily ever after, like in the movies."

She just looked at him. "Like in real life," she said

at last. "Movies and theater are illusions. I want the real thing."

He leaned down and touched her lips with a kiss as gentle as spring rain. "Is that real enough for you?" he asked.

"Yes," she whispered. "That's perfect."

Chapter Ten

*D*ear Addie, I'm in love with Lionel, but my mother says he's a bum because he didn't go to college and his hands are sometimes stained with grease and oil. Addie, Lionel works as an auto mechanic, so of course his hands are a little dirty now and then. I don't know why Mom won't give him a chance. He's kind and polite to her; he's wonderful to me. He makes my heart sing. Should I go ahead and marry him like my heart says to, or should I wait until I find the kind of man Mom says will earn a good living and make me happy? What do you think, Addie? Just sign me—Confused.

Dear Confused, take this from someone who knows what they're talking about: Marry the one you love. With luck, the two of you will sing a duet forever. Best Wishes, Addie.